THE OPEN UNIVERSITY

Arts: A Third Level Course
A361 SHAKESPEARE

BLOCK I

Henry IV

Parts 1 and 2

The Open University Press

The Open University Press
Walton Hall, Milton Keynes
MK7 6AA

First published 1983. Reprinted 1988

Designed by the Graphic Design Group of the Open University.

Printed in Great Britain by
Adlard & Son Limited, Letchworth, Hertfordshire

ISBN 0 335 11210 2

This text forms part of an Open University course. The complete list of units in the course appears on the back cover of this text.

For general availability of supporting material referred to in this text, please write to Open University Educational Enterprises Limited, 12 Cofferidge Close, Stony Stratford, Milton Keynes MK11 1BY, Great Britain.

Further information on Open University courses may be obtained from the Admissions Office, The Open University, PO Box 48, Walton Hall, Milton Keynes MK7 6AB.

1.2

Contents

Henry IV Part 1

Henry IV Part 2

Introduction to the Course

IN 1982, the year in which we began to write the material for this course, the Royal Shakespeare Company moved into its new London home at the Barbican. They opened, as this course does, with the two plays about Henry IV—a coincidence that was not planned by us, nor did the RSC take our intentions into account! But it was perhaps not quite a coincidence, because the RSC chose these two plays to mark such an auspicious occasion for reasons similar to those that made us choose them. Though they are not the most well-known of Shakespeare's plays they are at the centre of his achievement: they combine the events that shape history with the homeliest detail; they move us to horror and to laughter; their language is sometimes grandiloquently rich, sometimes of a transparent simplicity; above all they are superbly theatrical—by which I mean that to see these plays in the theatre is to be conscious that it is *theatre* (the physical presence and interaction of actors, movement, costume, voices, music, sounds and lights, the sense of a shared public occasion) which has brought the text to life.

Why then read the plays, if reading is bound to be such an incomplete experience? And if we read, must we always try to imagine the plays happening in some theatre of the mind? I would claim that those who read and those who stage the plays have an identical responsibility which is to *expound the text*. But though we have done our best to assert how essential is the *performance* of drama it is none the less impossible to ignore the considerable mutual hostility which exists between the people of the theatre and literary critics. It is a contest which the critics often duck, retreating guiltily under the onslaughts of the practitioners. The theatre complains that the critics are conservative, pedantic and sterile, and the critics complain that actors and producers distort or over-simplify the meaning of the texts. The theatre's claim that the plays were written for the stage and are lifeless without it seems to be unanswerable and anyone fortunate enough to have seen any of the plays well done will have found this proved on countless occasions. Yet one of our distinguished contributors, very much a person of the theatre, admits that no single production could simultaneously show all the profound complexity of certain scenes in *King Lear*, whilst the reader, unconfined by the physical restraints of the theatre, can apprehend a multitude of meanings and still have the capacity to be aware that much may remain beyond his or her understanding.

In this course we do not just pay lip service to performance. We are fortunate enough to be able to make the exploration of what happens between the page and the stage an integrated part of the task ahead of you. We should never lose sight of each play's need for theatre, but neither should we feel that what we are doing is second best. It is worth remembering that Shakespeare's plays went into print very soon after their first performances, and when all the plays were collected in the First Folio of 1623 after Shakespeare's death its preface was emphatically addressed 'To the great Variety of *Readers*'.

Shakespeare's status and reputation are unique and in some ways very odd. The very existence of the *Royal* Shakespeare Company suggests how much his work is part of the Establishment. Why should the plays not take their chance in the repertory as the work of other playwrights must? There is a growing body of complaint that the subsidies and patronage which make lavish production of Shakespeare's plays possible in Stratford, London and occasionally elsewhere starve other companies, and that the veneration of a playwright 367 years dead is one more symptom of the British malaise that makes us value a glorious past and invest too little in the future. Shakespeare has become part of the fabric of English nationalism: neither the day of his birth nor of his death is certain, but since both were within a few days of St George's Day, tradition has firmly established not just one but both dates as 23 April. John of Gaunt's famous lines about England in *Richard II* have been taken out of context almost since they were first written, and have come to be thought of as a lyrical equivalent to 'Rule Britannia'—forgetting of course that in the play from which they come England is not just this precious stone set in a silver sea but also 'leas'd out . . . like to a tenement or pelting farm . . . bound in with shame'. The RSC must have planned its productions of Henry IV long before the Falklands War blew up, but at a time when some of the worst elements of patriotism and militarism were raging it was salutary to see the idea of honour explored in the characters of Hotspur and Falstaff, and to watch a play which shows how much of value is sacrificed in the name of wise government.

'He was not of an age but for all times' wrote Ben Jonson shortly after Shakespeare's death. It was a large claim, but it has proved true. Why should so many people, from all over the world, assemble at some expense to sit for four hours in a purpose-built theatre that has cost millions of pounds, to watch a play written four hundred years ago about people who had already been dead two hundred years ? And why should we offer you this course ? There are many answers, among which 'celebration' and 'pleasure' are not the least. What we are *not* attempting—and what no intrinsically valuable modern production attempts either—are accurate and exclusive historical reconstructions. The ways that Shakespeare is alive in our time are something we intend to show as the course develops.

CPH

Study Material

The study material for Block I consists of the following:

THE CORRESPONDENCE TEXTS

TELEVISION

Programme 1	Henry IV Part 1,	I.2
	Henry IV Part 1,	II.4
	Henry IV Part 2,	V.5
Programme 2	Henry IV Part 1,	I.3
	Henry IV Part 1,	III.2
	Henry IV Part 2,	IV.5

PERFORMANCE CASSETTE

Cassette 5 (P),	Henry IV Part 2,	III.1
side A	Henry IV Part 2,	III.2.1–52
	Henry IV Part 2,	V.1.1–55
	Henry IV Part 2,	V.3
	Henry V,	II.3.1–26

RADIO

Programme 1 Shakespeare's Histories (by G. K. Hunter)

The set texts of the *Henry IV* plays are the Penguin New Shakespeare editions, edited by P. H. Davison.

Henry IV

Part 1

Prepared for the Course Team by P. N. Furbank

Introduction

CICELY Havely has already suggested in the Introduction to the Course some reasons why a course on Shakespeare may reasonably begin with study of his two *Henry IV* plays. They are, as she says, 'at the centre of his achievement'. Further, part of the reason for their continuing popularity has to do with the fact that they are about England and English history, so that for English audiences they are in a sense about ourselves.

But what the plays' popularity has much more to do with is—in a word—Falstaff. One had to wait till the novels of Dickens before meeting other such comic figures, capable to the same degree of walking off the boards or off the page into our imagination and lodging themselves there as a myth and a household word. There are many reasons for Falstaff's fascination, and one of them brings us back to the present course and the way that it is planned. For in this play, and especially in the Falstaff scenes, Shakespeare did something very original. He risked showing characters behaving, as it were, casually and 'off duty'—just being themselves, rather than performing moves in some rigidly laid-out plot. And you will find that in the next play that you will be studying, Shakespeare's late 'Roman' tragedy *Antony and Cleopatra*, he takes the method further. By this loosening up of the stage action we are given the illusion of getting to know Cleopatra, not just as a character in a plot but as we might know an acquaintance. We are given this same illusion with Falstaff. Indeed, it may not just be an accident that it should occur with these two characters: for both are professional fascinators and seducers, and both, in the context of their play, raise the issue of the conflicting claims of private life, and of the public life of honour and duty.

The *Henry IV* plays were written somewhere about 1596 to 1598. (The first part was entered in the Stationers' Register on 25 February 1598.) Shakespeare had previously produced six other history plays: *Henry VI* (which is in three parts), *Richard III*, *King John* and *Richard II*. And though the order of their writing did not follow the historical order of the reigns they depicted, the plays are full of echoes of one another, and one can detect in them an overall plot or theme. It is the theme of expiation, or of a guilt working itself out. For, as we are never allowed to forget in these plays, it was the deposition and murder of Richard II by Bolingbroke (the Henry IV-to-be) that was—so these plays would have us believe—the source of all the evils and conflicts of the ensuing century: the revolts of Bolingbroke's disaffected allies, and the later civil wars of the houses of York and Lancaster. The bitter closing words of *Richard II*, in which Bolingbroke banishes Sir Pierce of Exton for the murder of Richard II (a murder performed on his own instructions), is meant to ring in our ears throughout the Henry IV plays:

> They love not poison that do poison need,
> Nor do I thee: though I did wish him dead,
> I hate the murderer, love him murderéd.
> The guilt of conscience take thou for thy labour,
> But neither my good word nor princely favour:
> With Cain go wander through the shades of night,
> And never show thy head by day nor light.
> Lords, I protest, my soul is full of woe
> That blood should sprinkle me to make me grow:
> Come, mourn with me for that I do lament,
> And put on sullen black incontinent:
> I'll make a voyage to the Holy Land,
> To wash this blood off from my guilty hand . . .
>
> (*Richard II*, V.6.38–50)

According to the plot or theme running through Shakespeare's history plays, the guilt of Richard's death was only finally purged, and the evils and discords finally resolved, when the Lancastrian Henry Tudor (the Henry VII-to-be) defeated Richard III at Bosworth Field, ascended the throne, and united the warring houses by marrying Elizabeth of York. And, as may be perceived, this plot is flattering to the Tudors generally and hence to Queen Elizabeth, granddaughter of Henry VII and most successful of the Tudor despots. Shakespeare is writing of anarchy and civil wars in a period when, for the time being, England—at the cost of rigid government—seems stable, prosperous and united. (Or shall we say, *relatively* so; for as at all periods, it was beset by anxieties. See pp. 39–40.)

For further facts about the circumstances in which the *Henry IV* plays were written, their sources and Shakespeare's use of these, and their place in Shakespeare's work as a whole, you should consult Davison's helpful Introduction to the set text, and I shall work on the assumption that you will be reading this. But before that or anything else, I want you now to give the play itself a first reading. If you are not very familiar with Shakespeare you will probably find certain bits of the play obscure, simply because of the language: especially is this likely with the exchanges of wit in comedy scenes. The wit is predominantly a matter of puns and plays-upon-words; and even if these were easy to pick up for Shakespeare's original audience (which may not have been the case) they are bound to be difficult for us, four centuries later, when idioms and the meaning of words have changed. Thus, so as not to interrupt the flow of your first reading, you might do well to skate over the most obscure passages.

In reading, you should do all you can to picture the scenes as unfolding on a stage. Remember that the scenes run into one another very quickly, without elaborate scene-changes (indeed, quite often the 'scene 1', 'scene 2', etc., are later additions and do not appear in the earliest printed texts); hence one of the richest sources of effect in Shakespeare (and particularly so in this play, with its counterpointing of 'private' and 'public', of 'high-life' and 'low-life') is the contrast (comic, ironic or frightening) of a scene with its predecessor. Also, make a particular effort to visualize certain *tableaux*. The climax of the present play, the Battle of Shrewsbury, is—as you will find—composed of one extraordinary *tableau* after another—grotesque, heroic, comic or disquieting. With a little effort and practice you can learn to 'realize' such scenes very vividly, and this, of course, is one of the things that Shakespeare's language is designed to foster.

A word or two about *conventions*. The basic convention, by which 'serious' scenes are in blank verse and 'comic' scenes in prose is easily grasped, though I shall have more to say about it later. Note also the convention of the *soliloquy*, by which a character as it were steps out of the play, coming down to the front of the apron stage and entering into a closer relation with the *audience*.

Another convention to notice is the one according to which scenes are brought to an end by a rhyming couplet. It puts one vaguely in mind of music and the formal devices by which, in classical music, it is conveyed to us that a movement is coming to a close. In general, in Elizabethan drama, as often in Shakespeare, the couplet-ending has an epigrammatic or moralizing twist. But Shakespeare sometimes finds other, and very original and powerful, uses for it.

PNF

The Language of the Play

Introductory

We have made it part of the teaching strategy of this course that once or twice in the study of each play we will pause, and slow your study to a snail's pace to look in detail at some of the problems and more complex pleasures that Shakespeare's language involves. Language is inseparable from meaning and intention. The play is no less than its language—though, of course, when performed it may be more. Shakespeare's language will actually be the major subject of your study. What I want to do is reinforce the work of my colleagues by putting certain features of that language under the microscope from time to time.

Read again the King's opening speech in *1 Henry IV*. Use the notes and read it aloud, as 'dramatically' as you can. What is the King saying and why is he saying it like this?

He is reminding his court that the civil war is over and that it has been decided that the once opposing armies can prepare to march on a common enemy in a crusade. But Shakespeare is not just dressing up the minimum necessary information in gratuitous verbiage. First, he wants us to remember the peculiar horrors of civil war, and then he wants to impress on us that this is a king who believes he can fight for God.

The second part of the speech, from line 18 ('Therefore friends'), is more straightforward than the preceding lines, and before considering whether there are any reasons why this should be so, I want to look in some detail at the way in which the earlier part of the speech is put together.

Notice the succession of emphatic negatives at the beginning of lines 5, 7 and 8. The normal prose order (e.g. this soil shall not daub her lips any more) has been inverted to give them prominence. And they are followed in line 14 by an equally emphatically placed reversal or contradiction: 'Shall *now*'.

'No more' of what is eventually summed up in line 13 as 'civil butchery', but *now* not peace (which you might expect) but war against a common enemy: 'March all one way, and be no more opposed' (15). In this simple line is the gist of the matter.

It is the densely packed metaphors of Henry's speech that make it seem so 'dressed up' to us—a verbal equivalent of the king's robe of state compared with the mud-stained, workaday appearance that the messenger Blunt should present. Peace (line 2) is 'frighted' and is to be thought of as speaking of the 'new broils to be commenced in strands afar remote' in 'short-winded accents' (3–4). Pretending that an abstract quality like peace is a human being is called 'personification'. Look through the rest of the speech down to line 18 ('master') and identify what other abstractions or things are personified in a similar way.

In lines 5 and 6 the soil is seen as an unnatural mother of the kind more common in myth than in life who eats her own children—a figure that emphasizes the peculiar horror of *civil* war. (And see your editor's note.) But the same mother soil is herself abused, her fields channelled or trenched, her flowers bruised by 'hostile paces' (8–9). In lines 17–18 the 'edge of war, like an ill-sheathed knife' hardly seems to require the personification that the pronoun 'his' supplies. Surely 'its' would have done as well. *Yet every word is there for a purpose.* Here, the personification adds to the powerful suggestion that this war has had an evil life of its own, and that something even worse than individual suffering and death has been involved. This suggestion is strengthened in the difficult lines 9–11, where the conflict is compared to some vast and hideous conflict in the heavens themselves.

There is no such metaphoric elaboration in the second part of the speech beginning at line 18. And this is appropriate because King Henry wants his people to believe that their right and duty to deliver the Holy Land from infidels is *plain*. The contrast between the first and second parts of this speech thus illustrates an important principle: that Shakespeare's language varies according to his precise dramatic needs.

At a simple level this is of course ridiculously obvious. We all use different language for the expression of joy or grief. But in Shakespeare this principle is—quite literally—developed to a fine art.

We'll approach this question in wider terms and look at other verbal contrasts within the scene. King Henry is addressing his Council of War. Sir Walter Blunt is 'new lighted from his horse,/Stained with the variation of each soil' (63–4) and must present a bedraggled contrast to the rich garments of the King and his nobles. And this contrast makes visual the interruption the scene presents. For though Henry believes that the 'civil butchery' (13) is now at an end, and the country can be united in a crusade, he is immediately disillusioned by news of fresh fighting: a defeat in Wales (36–46) and an, at first, uncertain victory in the North (49–75). Compared with either part of Henry's opening speech, Westmorland's description of the fighting in Wales is plain words in plain order. Read it again to be sure of this. So Henry's elaborate diction isn't any kind of 'norm' for Shakespeare's works in general, for this play, this scene—or even for this character—as his concise response (47–8) confirms. And if the iteration of names and phrases like 'uneven and unwelcome' (50) and 'ever-valiant and approved' (54—another of those words which the modern reader may mistake: it meant 'well-tried') make Westmorland's next speech less clear, may not that be because the 'issue' of the battle is still 'Uncertain . . . any way', and so the quality of the language is reflecting the confusion of what is being said? Yet as in the King's first speech, the phrases on which all else depends stand out in their clarity:

> A sad and bloody hour (56)
> Uncertain of the issue any way (61)

Get these two points, and how everything else relates to them is not so important.

With these points in mind consider King Henry's speech at line 77 and in particular lines 85–8. How does the way in which Henry expresses the idea of the changeling child fit in with the rest of this scene? How would you characterize the tone of the phrase 'some night-tripping fairy'?

Did you, like the present writer, find yourself out of sympathy with what *seems* like incongruous prettiness and sentimentality? Amidst all this talk of war it seems completely out of place. Is it a touching glimpse of a private sorrow amidst the cares of state? But of course the character of a Prince of Wales *is* one of the cares of state, and ought not Henry to be doing something about it instead of merely talking about it so decoratively? The contrast in idiom is more clearly registered than its precise meaning. And in fact I was quite mistaken about the tone of these lines. There is certainly a shift—but not towards whimsy. Fairies in tutus are a Victorian invention. When this play was written its audience would not have thought of fairies as pretty at all, but as malevolent and sinister.

But how can you be expected to spot changes in attitude such as this where our modern point of view supplies a perfectly satisfactory reading? Your editors' notes will often help and we shall point out similar instances where we can which you should do your best to assimilate. But you can't spot every change and no one expects it. The director of this scene might find it easier to shape the moment in terms of the modern meaning rather than what was undoubtedly Shakespeare's original intention.

Turn back to the King's first speech. For what purpose does Shakespeare give him these words and not a simple prose statement to the effect that now the civil wars are over, he would like to mount a crusade?

You will perhaps have seen by now that Shakespeare wanted to make a more impressive statement than that would have been. Surely even a modern politician, making a comparable statement, would use all the rhetorical powers at his or her command. The public statement of issues of great importance is always an occasion that demands not simple, natural, colloquial language, but all the resources of language that the politician can muster. And that is what is happening here.

Shakespeare, however, had resources that are not available to the modern dramatist—or the modern politician for that matter. We are suspicious of over-elaborate rhetoric. We resist the manipulation of our feelings that such language seems to imply—and sometimes forget that simplicity or the deliberate use of homely, familiar language is itself a rhetorical ploy that can be just as manipulative. (Think of the politician who claims to be talking to us 'man to man'.) Shakespeare's audience expected a king to talk like an ideal king should—even though they probably all realized that real kings could never talk so well.

There will be much more to say later in the course about the constitution and capabilities of Shakespeare's audiences. But one thing it will be useful to think about from the beginning: from the lordlings to the groundlings they were better listeners than we are. They had to be.

Speech was far and away the most important form of communication for all occasions. This is not to say that everyone instantly picked up the precise meaning of everything he or she heard. But they would register the sonorities of the King's first speech, and respond to its elevated grandiloquence in a way that is perhaps more like catching the mood of music. Most important, neither Shakespeare nor any of his contemporaries ever believed that all poetry was above the heads of the many; and as far as we can tell (for ordinary people did not record their opinions on such matters) the many did not believe that poetry was not for them.

To summarize: I hope that our investigation of the language of the opening scene has demonstrated the following points.

(1) Everything in the play is there for a purpose: in this case, the opening lines establish a kingly tone and make vivid the horror of the civil wars that are not, as quickly becomes apparent, yet over.

(2) The quality of the diction is not uniform. The first part of the King's first speech is conspicuously more elaborate than much of what follows. And the two halves of the first speech are not so much difficulty followed by simplicity as *two distinct rhetorical strategies*.

(3) The language of the first eighteen lines is not naturalistic, but formal, even ritualistic: the diction dramatically appropriate to a significant moment in the affairs of state.

(4) This is elaborate and powerful poetry, not simply prose.

(5) Its mood or tone may be effectively clear even when its precise meaning is not.

CPH

Act I scenes 1 to 4

I propose now that we examine the first four scenes of the play fairly closely, and I should like you to re-read each of these scenes as we come to them (also studying the very helpful Notes in your text, pages 153–80).

Act I scene 1

In this first scene the King is holding an improvised Council, and he concludes by appointing a further Council meeting on Wednesday next at Windsor, and this—in a perfectly simple way—serves as a piece of dramatic construction, for it creates in us an expectation fulfilled in I.3. Notice, by the way, that (as often in the play) there is no indication where I.1 is taking place (see Davison's note p. 153). Nor, of course, is there any need for us to know. It reminds us, though, that the Elizabethan stage was not provided with realistic 'scenery', calling for 'scene changes' of the kind that take place behind a curtain. (Some time during this week's work you should listen to the cassette programmes on Shakespeare's Theatre, which discusses this and related points.)

As is very usual in any play, I.1 functions partly as an exposition, providing the audience with various essential facts. Observe, though (we have already touched on this point on page 12), that Shakespeare has done something rather ingenious. He shows the King holding a kind of stage-managed press-conference. He asks his kinsman the Earl of Westmorland to report what went on at the Council meeting of the previous evening and the decision taken there that, for the moment, the planned crusade to the Holy Land must be postponed. Now, presumably the King was at this meeting himself, so this report cannot be for his own information, and it must rather be for the benefit of the 'others' present at today's meeting. This is what I meant by its being stage-managed by the King. Similarly, Sir Walter Blunt has not arrived from the battlefield this very instant but perhaps a few hours ago, and the King with regal showmanship is exhibiting Blunt to the courtiers still in his mud-spattered clothes, to provide a *tableau* of loyalty and kingly graciousness ('Here is a dear, a true industrious friend . . . ' etc. I.1.62). Thus Shakespeare, needing to construct a scene of exposition for *our* sake has made this seem quite natural by the device of causing the King to arrange his own playlet or 'exposition-scene', for *his own* personal and political motives.

One comment may be added to the discussion of the King's speech on pages 11–13, *viz.* that a reason we might allege for its peculiar elaborateness is the realistic one that the speaker is *embarrassed*—as well he might be, considering the extreme uneasiness of his situation: a usurper, addressing men who may secretly be his enemies, and having a very insecure hold on his nation and title. Thus Henry is trying to do several different things at the same time in this speech: make a good impression, silence the accusations of his enemies, silence the accusations of his own conscience, appear kingly and pious with thoughts high above the vulgar throng, yet at the same time appear an efficient and alert politician in whom men can trust. As for his rueful contrasting of the heroic Hotspur with his own scapegrace son Hal, no doubt we are meant to take this partly as a sincere confession, and partly as a further skilful piece of statecraft; for by accusing Hal himself he is forestalling his critics and enemies. Prince Hal's bad reputation is not just a personal chagrin to the King but a dangerous weakness in his regime.

Let us pause before I.2 to make quite sure we know how the factions are composed in the current civil war, that is, who is on whose side, and why. The KING, of the House of Plantagenet, formerly Henry Bolingbroke, has been helped by Henry Percy, EARL OF NORTHUMBERLAND, and his son HARRY HOTSPUR, and by NORTHUMBERLAND'S brother Thomas Percy, EARL OF WORCESTER, to regain his estates, confiscated by Richard II; and when Bolingbroke has exploited this situation to seize the crown from Richard (thereby excluding Edmund, LORD MORTIMER, whom the deposed Richard wished to succeed him), they have condoned the usurpation. However, in the course of his efforts to subdue the rebellious Scots, led by the EARL OF DOUGLAS, and the rebellious Welsh, led by OWEN GLENDOWER, the KING has alienated his erstwhile allies, and a quarrel has broken out over the Scottish prisoners recently taken at the battle of Holmedon by HOTSPUR, who refuses to give them up to the KING unless the latter ransoms MORTIMER, who is HOTSPUR'S brother-in-law, from the hands of GLENDOWER. As a result of this quarrel, NORTHUMBERLAND, HOTSPUR and WORCESTER decide (see I.3) to throw in their lot with DOUGLAS, GLENDOWER and Richard Scroop, ARCHBISHOP OF YORK (who bears a grievance against the KING), to overthrow the KING. Amongst those who remain loyal to the KING are the EARL OF WESTMORLAND and SIR WALTER BLUNT.

Act I scene 2

The audience in Shakespeare's day was already aware, as a modern audience normally is, at least in a vague sort of way, that the royal father–son problem is going to be a central concern of the play. And in the very first line of I.2 the issue is made most vivid and actual; for the raffish-looking and grotesquely fat old knight Falstaff (instantly recognized by us, for we come to the theatre expecting to see Falstaff) addresses the King's eldest son, with cheerful effrontery, as 'lad'. The ensuing dialogue shows them as cronies and confederates, to whom nothing is sacred and between whom (in theory) no topic is barred. Their first topic of conversation is highway robbery, and nothing could better illustrate the condition of England under Henry than that a knight should be a part-time highway robber, or better illustrate Prince Hal's 'riotous' life than that he should consort with robbers, if not be one himself. But is he one himself? The question is obviously important but in fact has received differing answers in the past, some critics holding that Hal is quite clearly merely leading Falstaff on, for the fun of the thing, and never has the faintest intention of committing a highway robbery himself, other critics holding that he genuinely decides to try it, if only for sport ('Well then, once in my days, I'll be a madcap' I.2.140), until given the idea of even better sport by Poins.

Re-read the scene, asking yourself what your own view is.

I will now give you my view, which corresponds to neither of the above. It is that we are not supposed to know, or be able to decide, whether or not Hal ever contemplates crime. This is part of the fascination of the scene, that we are fooled and baffled by Hal, as Hal and Falstaff fool and baffle each other; and in this we resemble the people of England, who also do not know what to think of the rumours they hear. (Note that the fact that Hal eventually gives the money back—see II.4—does not conclusively prove his innocence.)

Another aspect of their conversation is Falstaff's interest in what Hal will do when he is king. He pleads jokingly for royal lenience towards enterprising men like robbers, whose 'resolution' ought not to be discouraged by old-fashioned bugbears such as the Law. He also pricks up his ears when Hal seems to be promising in due course to make him a judge. This theme, presented purely in joke-terms here, grows in importance and literalness as the play, and its sequel, proceed. Falstaff believes he has much to gain from corrupting Hal.

Notice, too, the particular line of argument used by Falstaff when he is egging him on to crime: he appeals to 'manhood', 'good fellowship' and royal 'blood' (I.2.137–9) and to the 'resolution' of such as himself and Gadshill. They are generous virtues which, we remind ourselves, are not so far off those that King Henry praises in Hotspur and whose lack he laments in Hal. Falstaff's pretence that he himself is a pious Puritan seduced and ruined by the daredevil rascal Hal reinforces the same line of attack. Thus one of the points that the play seems to be making is that virtues like 'resolution' and boldness are only virtues if used to the right end. We shall have doubts suggested to us about Hotspur's virtues, too, from this point of view. For Hotspur, though a dazzling figure, is a total egotist, and hence his gallantry is of no value to anyone but himself. He is a disastrous ally, and would have been an even more disastrous king. The *Henry IV* plays, we shall find, are much concerned, at a deep level, with the questions 'What makes a good king?' and 'As the fruit of what experiences did Prince Hal become the accomplished and successful monarch Henry V?'

Finally, let us examine Prince Hal's speech 'I know you all . . . ' (I.2.193–215). In discussing I.1, I was at some pains to give realistic explanations for what might be regarded as merely 'conventional'. I will now do the opposite and remind you that this speech of Hal's is a *soliloquy* and that it is important to bear in mind the nature of the soliloquy convention. We are not to think of Hal as merely talking to himself in this speech. We are to picture him (as I said on page 10) as stepping out of the action of the play and taking the audience into his confidence—a convention as important in Elizabethan drama as the convention by which a nineteenth-century novelist like George Eliot uses a fictional 'narrator', who similarly stands outside the action of the novel to tell the reader what to think.

To grasp the convention is important, but of course this takes us only a very little way. What is much more important is what Shakespeare makes of the convention, and this is a complex matter.

We can perhaps agree on one thing: the soliloquy, following as it does on a scene of relaxed comedy, gives us a considerable shock and sets our minds running on all sorts of possibilities. It is a most stirring moment. P. H. Davison, in his Introduction to the set text (p. 20) says: '. . . in the theatre the moment passes quickly . . . and the speech is forgotten'. I find this a surprising remark. The moment seems to me very difficult to forget. It forms part, after all, of our very first introduction to Hal and Falstaff, and thus has considerable prominence; and it sets up a tension, I suggest, which continues throughout this play and its successor—an uncertainty as to how sincere and spontaneous Hal is being at any time. In Falstaff's company he is, evidently, being 'himself' to some extent and is enjoying low life in Eastcheap for its own sake. But to *what* extent? And how much are both Hal and Falstaff, in the midst of their fun, cold-bloodedly scheming and trying to trick one another? This is a question that Shakespeare is continually jogging us with throughout the play.

We drew an analogy between the Elizabethan soliloquy convention and the use of a fictional 'narrator' in nineteenth-century novels who tells the reader what to think. Here again what is important is how a great novelist like George Eliot or Dickens *uses* the convention. In reading *Middlemarch* or *Great Expectations* we soon become aware that the narrator is not really just standing outside the story. A much subtler game is being played by the author. We keep having to decide how much we can trust even the 'narrator's' account of events, and to speculate about what the 'narrator' may be up to.

In the same way, we find ourselves questioning the account of his motives that Hal gives us in his soliloquy. Are we to take it as a true account? Is this the sole or main thought in Hal's mind throughout his Eastcheap activities? If so, can he hope to bring off such a gamble—can he really hope to 'redeem' himself ultimately in this way? In life, do consequences work like this? If not, what are we meant to conclude about Hal's character? The questions multiply; and it becomes plain that the use of the soliloquy convention here is not meant to simplify our responses to the play (as when the villain in a Victorian melodrama hisses his foul purposes in an 'aside'), but on the contrary to complicate and enrich them.

The soliloquy convention is non-realistic. We are not meant to suppose that Hal is, at this moment, overheard talking to himself. But that does not mean that his soliloquy cannot be true to life. A help in defining the kind of 'truth to life' involved might be to consider Winston Churchill in the 1930s. It is clear that throughout the political and international vicissitudes of the 1930s, and above all the growing threat from Nazi Germany, Churchill was constructing a scenario (and causing others to construct a scenario) according to which the nation would eventually turn to him as a saviour and as the 'man of the hour'. His conduct suggests this very plainly, yet it may well be that he never put the idea to himself, let alone to others, in so many words; and if so, the fact, though true, could not be portrayed by a dramatist in 'realistic' fashion, whereas it could be conveyed by a non-realistic device like the soliloquy.

This leads us to the question, how shall we evaluate the strategy or 'ploy' outlined by Hal in his soliloquy (that of making oneself seem degenerate so that one's 'redemption' shall be all the more amazing and dazzling), as compared with the one recommended by the King, in his interview with Hal in III.2 (that of spacing out your public appearances, so that when they occur they make the maximum of impact)? Please re-read III.2.29–91. At first sight the ploys appear to be directly opposite ones, but further reflection soon shows us that this is not the case. Indeed the King and Hal agree on what is perhaps the most fundamental point.

What is this point?

It is that, in their view, it is essential to preserve the *mystique* of kingship. A king or prince must make himself an object of mystery: he must contrive to appeal to his subjects' imagination and superstition. The only serious difference between the King and Hal is as regards the best means to this end—whether it is best done by restricting your personal appearances in general (the King's plan) or by restricting your appearances in the guise of prince (Hal's plan).

I said that one of the many questions that Hal's soliloquy raises in our minds is, was Hal's scheme for his career a practicable one: can you hope to control events in such a way? Well, as the play progresses, it begins to appear that Shakespeare gives the answer 'Yes'. For at the approach of the battle of Shrewsbury, Prince Hal emerges, in Churchillian fashion, as the 'man of the hour', astonishing all observers, enemy and friend, with his transformation into demigod-like hero (see IV.1). And, plainly, the impact he makes at this time is enormously increased by the fact that it *is* a transformation. The sunlit radiance of the warrior Hal is enhanced, just as he said it would be, by the contrast of this 'bright metal' with the 'sullen ground' (I.2.210) of his raffish past. (I shall return to this scene later.) Again, at the end of *2 Henry IV*, Hal—in a moment as startling, and in a way shocking, to us as that of his first soliloquy—turns off Falstaff with words of icy contempt:

> I know thee not old man: fall to thy prayers . . . (*2 Henry IV*, V.5.50)

A colleague comments: 'Is "icy contempt" the only tone in which these words can be uttered? Does it not depend a lot on the actor and his particular conception of Hal?'

Can you think of a possible alternative reading?

The only alternative that occurs to me is a tone of kingly aloofness—as though Hal really *has* almost forgotten who Falstaff was.

Thus, the scheme of conduct Hal announced early on has been fully executed. Nor, taken by surprise though we must be by this stern denouement, can we complain that we have not been warned.

Will you now read pages 17–20 of P. H. Davison's Introduction?

Excellent as this Introduction is in some respects, I find that I disagree with almost everything that Davison says about Hal's soliloquy. Some of my reasons will appear from the foregoing. (Why should he refer to Shakespeare as 'bending the convention'? Artistic conventions are there to be 'bent', that is, exploited; that is what they exist for.) But the best way of summarizing my objections is to say that Davison sentimentalizes Shakespeare. He appears to assume that Shakespeare *must* want us to think well of Prince Hal and of Hotspur, and that when certain things that Hal and Hotspur say shock us, we must look for excuses. (They were very young at the time, etc. etc.) The assumption seems to me quite unnecessary, indeed to be definitely false, for Shakespeare never 'takes sides' or invites us to become the partisan of one or other of his characters or the cause they stand for. Shakespeare may be suggesting, or anyway allows us to conclude, that some such devious conduct as Hal's is necessary to successful kingship but we must not assume he is asking us to like Hal any the better for it.

See which of us you agree with, or if you agree with either. The issue between us is one that, in different shapes, you will come up against often in this course.

A digression on blank verse

It might be useful at this point to add something to Graham Martin's discussion of blank verse (see Course Guide). In regard to the *Henry IV* plays a rather obvious consideration suggests itself. The business of statesmanship and of courts of justice is conducted in formal and artificial language—a 'high' language, intended to be expressive of courtesy and ceremony and ideal values. It is so even now and was much more so in Shakespeare's day and in the Middle Ages. We have only to think of the phrasing of legal statutes and charters, for instance Magna Charta:

> John, by the grace of God, king of England, lord of Ireland, duke of Normandy and Aquitaine, count of Anjou, to the archbishops, bishops, abbots, earls, barons, justiciars, foresters, sheriffs, reeves, servants, and all bailiffs and his faithful people, greeting! Know that by the suggestion of God and for the good of our soul and those of all our predecessors and of our heirs, to the honour of God and the exaltation of holy church . . . etc.

So, when in Shakespeare's plays kings converse with courtiers or rival lords it is, in a sense, no more than strict realism that they should speak in high-flown and artificial fashion. Of course, I do not mean that kings spoke in blank verse. What I mean, rather, is that, just because blank verse is a convention, it does not mean it is a meaningless convention. *In its very conventionality* it can be suggestive of other conventions; and I think it is so here, in the *Henry IV* plays. (And this is a quite different point from the one that I shall be making later, that, artificial though blank verse be, Shakespeare can make it intensely suggestive of natural speech and of the temperamental idiosyncracies of different speakers. There are many different ways, almost no end to them, in which blank verse can be made expressive.)

There was a particular reason for stressing that, by its very conventionality, blank verse can be suggestive of other conventions. It is that the initial *datum* of *1 Henry IV*, the fact on which the whole plot turns, is that Prince Hal hates, or appears to hate, order and ceremony, the 'play-acting' of statesmanship and the solemnities of justice. It is his father's, the King's, great complaint against him, and it is an idea that Hal does everything in his power to foster. Of course we have his Act I soliloquy to reflect on, and it may be that Hal's dislike of public play-acting is itself a piece of play-acting and hypocrisy. Alerted by this soliloquy we shall watch Hal with suspicion and, as we see him and Falstaff amusing themselves at the expense of ceremony, and playing the fool with a mock-throne, mock-sceptre and mock-pompous royal speeches, we shall be wondering which of the two is the more deeply tricking the other. Nevertheless, that Hal despises order and ceremony does seem to have some truth in it; in a certain mood, at least, he does genuinely relish all kinds of disorder. And thus part of the contrast we are meant to feel between these prose scenes of Hal and Falstaff and the verse scenes of King Henry and his lords is the contrast between spontaneity and conventionality. The one rule observed by Hal and Falstaff is that they shall be *ready*—should have on the instant a witty rejoinder or a witty fantasy. Thus, whether or not we can always follow their wit-combats, the mere speed and inventiveness of their word-play is significant; the point comes across that this wild improvisation is, for them, freedom, whereas the life of ceremony and order is servitude.

Act I scene 3

Henry's opening speech in this scene again seems, at first, rather difficult. However, if you will look at the notes to it in your edition the difficulty should largely disappear. As P. H. Davison points out, when Henry says 'I will from henceforth rather be myself' (I.3.5), he means 'I will from now on be my kingly self, as opposed to my ordinary and natural self (which is gentle and compliant)'. This idea of a gap between a king's two identities allies itself later in the play with the question whether a usurper like Henry is truly a king at all, or whether his kingship may be merely a borrowed coat—a question given fantastic expression on the battlefield of Shrewsbury, when the field is full of mock-Henrys (knights dressed in his coats).

Further, we sense that the notion of Henry's two selves is placed here as a contrast and comment on the problem of *Hal's* various selves. The question of whether or not the victorious party is 'two-faced', as treacherous as the traitors, will undermine the audience's confidence in their victory.

The contrast which ensues in this sense between the fear-ridden and careworn king, cajoling or threatening his erstwhile confederates, and the vivid, impetuous and high-spirited Hotspur, concerned for one thing only, his personal honour and glory, is, I think you will agree, extremely telling. And it is all the more so by dint of that other implicit contrast, between the simple-minded Hotspur and the quick-witted and devious Hal displayed to us in the preceding scene.

The scene illustrates a talent in which, it is generally agreed, Shakespeare was unique among his contemporary dramatists: I mean, his power to mould blank verse for the creation of character. Consider the following (I.3.236–48):

Hotspur Why, look you, I am whipped and scourged with rods,
Nettled, and stung with pismires, when I hear
Of this vile politician Bolingbroke.
In Richard's time—what do you call the place?
A plague upon it, it is in Gloucestershire.
'Twas where the madcap Duke his uncle kept—
His uncle York—where I first bowed my knee
Unto this king of smiles, this Bolingbroke—
'Sblood, when you and he came back from Ravenspurgh—
Northumberland At Berkeley Castle.
Hotspur You say true.
Why, what a candy deal of courtesy
This fawning greyhound then did proffer me!

It is amazing how recognizable and three-dimensional a character emerges from the very texture and movement of this verse, with its disjointed crescendo, full of impatient self-interruptions—the emotions of the speaker travelling faster than the intellect. Observe, too, that Hotspur only speaks in these self-revealing accents when he is at the height of his rage—the rage he perhaps deliberately works himself up into. (You are not aware of the *man* Hotspur in that earlier speech of his, 'Revolted Mortimer' (I.3.93–111), which is merely a fine set-piece of Elizabethan poetic rhetoric. By which I do not mean to suggest that it has no dramatic *function.* For it evokes very powerfully Hotspur's general attitude, which draws a stark contrast between the living energies of courageous men—energies so grand as to put mere Nature in the shade and cause the river Severn to hide its head—and 'bare and rotten policy', the frowsty activities of mere politicians.)

By the end of this scene there is not much left for us to learn about Hotspur. His only real grievance against Henry is a personal one, the fact that his honour is offended by Henry's treatment of his kinsman Mortimer. It becomes plain that his machiavellian father and uncle consider him a fool, though a valuable asset none the less, and are using him for their own ends. Anyway, a glorious death is all he asks for. He is a brilliant chivalric figure, belonging to an older society or to medieval romance, not a fit person to resolve the complex problems facing the nation. Kingship would call for other qualities.

Act II scene 1

I should like you now to perform a slightly laborious exercise. It is to work through II.1, with the aid of the Notes in your edition, doing your best to understand *every word, phrase* and *allusion.* I have several reasons for asking this. The first is that, having done this little exercise, you should have gained confidence over the 'obscurity' problem and have sensed that there is a kind of skill or tact to be learned in reading Shakespeare, and especially Shakespearian wit. Not *every* difficult allusion or pun needs, in fact, to be followed up: the essential, rather, is to grasp the *drift* and *tone* of what is going on. My second reason is that this scene, though at first sight merely a piece of 'local colour', is actually exceedingly important. And my third reason is that the scene, taken in conjunction with I.2, provides us with a detective puzzle, interesting for its own sake and also of some significance for the play at large.

There is not much difficulty, I think, in getting the drift of the opening section of this scene: that is, the Carriers bustling about by lantern-light in the inn yard, grumbling at their night's accommodation and shouting for the ostler. You could even make a rough guess at the obscurer phrases, like 'put a few flocks in the point' (put some flock or wool in the saddlebow), or 'that is the next way to give poor jades the bots' (that is the nearest way to give poor broken-down horses worms). But, just for practice, I'd like you, as I have said, to work through the section phrase by phrase, with the help of the Notes, and get the sense quite clear.

What is the point of the next section, the conversation between the Carriers and Gadshill? Well, plainly it is that the Carriers instantly suspect Gadshill of being what he is—a highwayman—and fob him off, telling him the time wrongly and refusing to lend him their lanterns. (Though they are naive enough to mention, apparently in Gadshill's hearing, that the gentlemen in the inn have 'great charge', that is, valuable possessions.)

But now for what is, from a language point of view, the most difficult section: the exchange between the Chamberlain (or inn-servant) and Gadshill. Study the Notes and make up your mind to understand every word of this brief scene, in so far as this is possible. (In fact, commentators disagree about the meaning of several phrases, in particular the phrase 'O-yeas'.) It might be a good idea if you actually, laboriously, wrote out a paraphrase of this section (II.1.49–98). I will make a beginning of one myself:

Chamberlain 'Ready', as the pickpocket says. [There is a pun on 'hand'—a pickpocket has his hand ready at all times.]

Gadshill You might just as fairly say 'Ready as the chamberlain says'. For the only difference between being a chamberlain and being a pickpocket is the difference between supervising other people's work and doing the work yourself. You show them the way. [There is a pun on 'plot': as meaning (i) plan or method, and (ii) conspiracy.] . . .

Line 70

Here we come to a sentence that I am a little surprised is not more commented on in the Notes to your edition.

Gadshill . . . Tut, tut, there are other boon-companions involved whose identity you would never have guessed and who condescend to lend their prestige to our 'profession' for the fun of it, and who, if the thing came to the ears of the authorities, would be sure to smooth matters over and satisfy the injured parties, for the sake of their own reputation.

It seems plain that Gadshill is here referring to Prince Hal himself (someone so grand that the chamberlain would never have dreamed of his being involved). And I would have thought that the word 'night' a few lines later ('Nay, by my faith, I think you are more beholding to the night than to fern-seed for your walking invisible') must be a pun on 'knight', that is, an allusion to Falstaff.

The rest of Gadshill's confidences to the chamberlain go right to the heart of the play and of the extraordinary situation in England that it depicts or hints at. Gadshill, a highwayman is in league with the Prince and his friends and the highest in the land; and, according to Gadshill's account (II.1.70–83)—though of course we need not necessarily believe him—these highly-placed people not only play at highway robbery but, in a metaphorical and more serious sense, are playing the highwayman towards the nation, robbing her and corrupting her judges at will. Short of treason, you could hardly have greater 'disorder' than this.

From a painting attributed to Buss: William Downton as Falstaff, with John Cooper and John Balls in Henry IV Part II, Drury Lane, 1842. (Harvard Theatre Collection)

Acts II and III in general

From this point on my commentary will be less systematic. For the main part we may regard Acts II and III as the working out of the themes, relationships and possibilities, especially comic possibilities, set up in Act I, and this part of the play, which contains some of Shakespeare's most famous scenes of comedy, is very clear in its construction. Thus, there is less need to guide you through it scene by scene. One or two points need special discussion, however. You should especially pay attention to the 'role-exchanging' scene (II.4.366–470), in which Falstaff and Hal rehearse Hal's forthcoming interview with his father—the role of king being first adopted by Falstaff and then by Hal. It will be noticed that, in this incident, the theme of role-playing, touched on earlier, is explored very thoroughly and from a variety of different angles. In Act I we came across the idea of kingliness as a separable personality, to be put on or taken off like a garment, and this is evidently glanced at in Falstaff's improvised crown, sceptre and throne. Again, we are reminded of the ancient Christmastide tradition of the Lord (or King) of Misrule, the mock-king who directs horseplay and unruly festivities. Such a reversal of social order still survives in the army custom that on Christmas Day the officers serve the 'men' at table; and in a larger sense such a reversal is, of course, what seems to be existing in Henry IV's England—with the Prince of Wales consorting with robbers, the courts of law corrupted, and the country at civil war. But further, we cannot help remembering that, according to his own confession, Hal's own 'low life' activities are a form of role-playing and part of a scheme for future self-advancement in the nation's eyes. (Re-read his soliloquy at the end of I.2.) Nor, when in III.2, we see the serious interview with the King which is parodied here, can we fail to ask ourselves if Hal is merely acting a part there too. Finally, as Mistress Quickly reminds us ('O Jesu, he doth it as like one of those harlotry players as ever I see', II.4.388–9), what we in the audience are witnessing is a troupe of actors, men professionally employed to dress up in royal or other borrowed clothes. It is common for Shakespeare to undercut his own stage illusion in this way, and by so doing he suggests a whole array of subtle reflections on the human condition: that social and political relationships are based on voluntary or involuntary illusion, and that private relationships are no less so, etc. You will come across a further example in *Antony and Cleopatra*. (There is, by the way, a not-quite-dissimilar joke—or so one could interpret it—when Shakespeare makes Hotspur express such withering contempt for mere *poets* and their 'mincing poetry' (III.1.123–9).)

Another scene to study with much attention is the one which takes place at Owen Glendower's castle (if it is a castle) in Wales. It is an unexpected joke (and, if you think of it, a very good one) that Owen Glendower should turn out to be much further gone in glory-seeking and bravado than Hotspur himself: indeed the Welsh wizard and warrior, with his mysterious and awe-inspiring reputation, is a crashing dinner-table bore. Hotspur is most unimpressed, blithely pooh-poohing the old windbag's ridiculous tall stories, till the latter nearly bursts with apoplexy. It is a moment of farce, modulating again unexpectedly, with the entry of the young wives, into a moment of romantic comedy (a little reminiscent of *Twelfth Night*). The young people bicker amicably, Mortimer's Welsh wife sings an ancient ditty; it is a moment of repose and relaxation. Shakespeare, by the time of the *Henry IV* plays, is an immensely resourceful dramatist, and, fittingly in a play with such a vast and nationwide canvas as this, he presents many different 'atmospheres'. We are a long way here from the elderly and hag-ridden atmosphere of the court, or again from the riotous atmosphere of the Boar's Head.

The end of this whole 'movement' of the play (II and III), and the hinge to the final movement (IV and V), comes with the flurry of activity leading up to the battle of Shrewsbury. It is epitomized in the final couplet of III, spoken by Falstaff:

> Rare words! Brave world! Hostess, my breakfast, come!
> O, I could wish this tavern were my drum.

This couplet is curiously fascinating. It is partly that the word 'drum' is used in a way that seems so 'right' and yet takes a little explaining. Actually, P. H. Davison (see his note) seems to me to make unnecessary difficulties, for surely there is no problem in understanding 'drum' as a metaphor for military activity in general? However, this does not exhaust the meaning we find packed into 'I could wish this tavern were my drum'. For the word also brings to mind the idea of *beating* a drum, that is to say making a noise in the world, and I think this meaning is also present. Falstaff plainly would like to make a noise in the world. He is excited by the new turn of events and will eat his breakfast with zest. His phrase 'Brave world!' is not wholly ironical, for he scents possibilities of profit and renown, and indeed he will achieve and earn a reputation as a hero, though by rascally means. On the other hand, he dearly loves his comforts, and even more dearly loves his own skin. Thus two contrary feelings are running through this compressed and powerful couplet, and Falstaff is *not* merely saying 'I wish it were not all happening and I could be left to eat my breakfast and drink my sack in peace'; he is saying something much more complex and interesting.

PNF

The Language of the Play

Act II scene 4

The text is obviously incomplete without performance, yet it contains the signals necessary for its own fullest interpretation. Several of our television programmes are about how actors discover the resources of the text, and watching them and listening to the performance cassettes will, we hope, enable you to make your own private reading more of a performance. I don't mean that you must aspire to be an actor. But an alertness to how the text may ask to be acted will considerably enhance your understanding of its meaning.

But it is not enough to be able to respond to the text instinctively. You have to learn to articulate your response—even though the effect of such prodigious articulation as these scenes set before us with all their rich, chaotic wealth of verbal invention may be to strike one dumb with amazement. It is immediately obvious that the language of II.4 is no less elaborate than the examples of stately rhetoric that we considered at the beginning of the play and yet it could hardly be more different. It is as if we were in another country, with another language—and to say that of course is to recognize that the way Shakespeare allocates different idioms is an essential part of the drama.

Although the notes to this scene will have shown how much scholarship has been devoted to revivifying long-lost jokes, very little attention has ever been paid to the rhetoric of scenes such as these. There is little established terminology which we can use to analyse its effects. But we must not be deterred.

A highly conscious awareness of language is part of the characterization of both Hal and Falstaff and several of their cronies. It is what this scene first draws our attention to in the otherwise gratuitous episode of the joke which Hal and Poins play on Francis the harassed drawer (ll. 1–80).

Look at Hal's first long speech (ll. 1–32) and identify those parts of it which confirm his claim to have become 'so good a proficient in one quarter of an hour that I can drink with any tinker in his own language during my life'.

He is like a student of the drawers' language—an activity which has an obvious bearing on how we assess his divided life. The phrases printed in inverted commas towards the end of the speech are direct quotations from the kind of phrases an inn servant must be constantly using. Earlier, the phrases 'dyeing scarlet', 'Hem' and 'Play it off' are part of the drawers' slang and of course this is an occasion for a virtuoso display of funny accents and comic business. But Hal is also quoting the drawers between lines 8 and 14. It is Tom, Dick and not Harry of course but Francis who have sworn on their salvation, and called Hal 'King of courtesy', a 'Corinthian'—which means here nothing specific but is a grandiose name for an heroic roisterer—'a good boy' (which Hal finds ironic) and so on.

But if we are inclined to think well of Hal for studying the language of his future subjects, the joke he plays on the simple Francis—who has 'fewer words than a parrot' (l. 96)—will modify our benevolence, for he uses his own verbal agility to dazzle and confuse the poor creature. As the pace becomes more furious Hal's words have less and less meaning, but they sound as if they ought to mean something, and the drawer, constantly being yelled for by Poins in the next room, simply cannot keep up. It is a display of Hal's effortless patrician superiority and although it is undoubtedly very funny I think we are also a little disturbed by such an unkind waste of talent. And perhaps we should also reflect on the significance of a joke about a man trying to be in two places at once.

From this, with no apparent connection, Hal moves into an equally talented and high-spirited parody of Hotspur and the scene eventually culminates in the funny and searching double imitations of the King and Prince.

Falstaff begins by taking the King's part—in both senses of that phrase. Yet before he begins he limbers up as it were with a few lines 'in King Cambyses' vein', that is, in the exaggerated manner of older historic dramas. Shakespeare delighted in parodying bombastic rhetoric such as Falstaff imitates here (ll. 384 and 386–7) and the joke is a vivid indication of the verbal sophistication Shakespeare was able to rely on in his audience. But Falstaff's impersonation of the

King does not continue in this vein.

Read his two speeches as King between lines 390 and 420 and try to identify not just their tone, but what idiomatic features give them that tone.

This is not an imitation of Henry IV as we have seen him, though it is worth looking back to the King's own admission of fatherly regrets at I.1.77–90. Falstaff's King is not so lyrical. He is platitudinous and sententious. A bore who if he were real would make his chidden son wriggle with embarrassment at such commonplace sanctimoniousness. Falstaff's version of the King is a lack-lustre figure who depends on proverbs to express his moral wisdom ('For though the camomile . . . ', 'a thing . . . known to many in our land by the name of pitch'; 'if then the tree may be known by the fruit . . . '). He is wordy, dull and prosaic ('That thou art my son I have partly thy mother's word . . . '), in a word the heavy father. And yet part of the comedy depends on the incompleteness of the parody. It is not only funny because it is Falstaff who is speaking these words; some of the words would be impossible in such a King or such a father: 'Harry, now I do not speak to thee in drink, but in tears'. Such a virtuous father would *never* be drunk—but Falstaff often is. And the question 'Shall the sun of Heaven prove a micher and eat blackberries?' depends for its humour on colloquial and homely words like 'micher' and 'blackberries' which are part of Falstaff's natural idiom being said in a tone of lordly disparagement.

Just as we have seen that Shakespeare's more obviously poetic elaborations are never mere decoration so we can now see an excellent example of how comedy here is far from being mere light relief, but continues and develops the themes of the play. What is more, just as we have seen how Shakespeare takes pains to make sure that essential information is expressed with conspicuous simplicity (except, conversely, where ambiguity seems to have been part of his purpose, as in the case of Hal's share in the robbery) so in the comic scenes certain key points will stand out from the mass of comic verbal ingenuity and are no less serious for their funny settings. Thus here Falstaff's King asks 'shall the son of England prove a thief and take purses?' We are aware that Hal's feelings about Falstaff are ambiguous, but does not this question disturbingly suggest that Falstaff is not as single-minded in his affection for Hal as we might at first think? Surely by the end of the second, reversed dialogue (when Hal 'plays' his father) we may be aware of a next to open hostility between them:

Falstaff Banish plump Jack, and banish all the world.
Prince Hal I do, I will.

Perhaps the knocking that follows (at l. 466) breaks a tense silence.

And yet in the television workshop you will see that other meanings can be found here, and the best may be that which manages to convey most possible interpretations simultaneously. The lesson of that experience in the studio was that one should never be content to rest with the first satisfactory explanation one finds. It may be possible to go on discovering further layers of meaning.

But look at Hal's impersonation of his father and contrast it with Falstaff's. What special verbal characteristics do you notice (ll. 434–46)?

After the sentence 'Thou art violently carried away from grace' Hal naturally enough directs his attack away from himself and towards Falstaff, who had not blamed Hal half so colourfully. Hal's language is characterized by the inventiveness of its abuse. His speech is mainly a string of insulting appellations, the first group (down to 'belly') referring to Falstaff's grossness, the second to his symbolic role, or what he stands for. (See Notes and this block pages 21 and 58.) The speech is also for the most part a string of rhetorical questions—questions, that is, which either do not need an answer or, because of the way in which they are put, supply their own. The speech ends with no fewer than six questions all beginning 'wherein' and culminating in the nonsensical but devastating 'wherein worthy, but in nothing?' Where questions come so thick and fast do we not also ask whether these are questions that Hal is asking himself as well as pretending to be his father asking? And yet if Hal at least half-believes that Falstaff is 'worthy . . . in nothing' why does his impersonation of his father sound so very much like the kind of language that he and Falstaff enjoy together? The speeches of both in their own persons during this scene are characterized by inventive abuse, strings of energetic variations referring to the same thing, and rhetorical questions. Though it is crude, their language has its own robust poetry, and they exercise themselves in it as they might in a sport, constantly and consciously striving after a new record.

> *Prince Hal* . . . This sanguine coward, this bedpresser, this horse-back-breaker, this huge hill of flesh—
> *Falstaff* 'Sblood, you starveling, you elf-skin, you dried neat's-tongue, you bull's-pizzle, you stock-fish! O for breath to utter what is like thee! You tailor's-yard, you sheath, you bow-case, you vile standing tuck!
> *Prince Hal* Well, breathe awhile, and then to it again . . . (ll. 237–44)

Poetic language is not defined by the use of poetic metre. Though prose, the language of these scenes frequently has its own rhythms, and of course its vocabulary, though quite different in range from that of the blank-verse scenes, it is at least as varied and resourceful.

It is largely because Shakespeare here relies so heavily on the riches of colloquial English that these scenes are sometimes so difficult to understand. The King and the nobles in the verse-scenes are given a more literary, and hence, relatively speaking, a more permanent language. But the characters in these scenes are given a highly wrought imitation of the spoken language which, by its very nature, enjoys no such stability. Even in a short life-time you can be aware of how quickly the spoken language changes. So some of the words that are strangest to us may have sounded as homely and familiar to an Elizabethan audience as the word 'blackberries' (twice used so vividly in this scene) still does today.

At line 124 Falstaff says

> If manhood, good manhood, be not forgot upon the face of the earth, then am I a shotten herring.

This colloquial construction ('if . . . then . . . ', a conditional imprecation addressed to oneself) survives in English only in a limited number of fixed forms such as 'If . . . (something unlikely), then I'm the Queen of Sheba' meaning emphatically that the speaker refuses to do or admit something.

Re-read the scene from Falstaff's entrance at line 110 to the Hostess's entrance at line 276 where Falstaff presents his version of the ambush which we know the Prince and Poins have set up, and look for other examples of this same 'If . . . then I' construction.

Falstaff's language *is* the man, and this distinctive feature of his idiom tells us a lot about him. It is used very frequently in this episode: at lines 113 ('Ere'), 124, 131, and in a simpler form at 147 ('I am a rogue if I drunk today'), 159, 165,

174, 180, 182, 188, and another simple form at 202 ('Seven . . . or I am a villain else') and 235. Let us look at three examples in more detail:

1 If I do not beat thee out of thy kingdom with a dagger of lath, and drive all thy subjects afore thee like a flock of wild geese, I'll never wear hair on my face more. (ll. 131–4)

2 . . . if I fought not with fifty of them I am a bunch of radish. (ll. 180–1)

3 If reasons were as plentiful as blackberries, I would give no man a reason upon compulsion . . . (ll. 235–6)

Unlike the modern usage these are not all negative. The first is an assertion that Falstaff, like the Vice in the old plays, *will* triumph over the Prince—and he'll stake his virility on it. In the second the fact that Falstaff is obviously *not* a bunch of radishes (proverbially lean fare) is supposed to prove that he *did* fight with fifty men. Both, like the other instances of this form here, are plain absurdities. And the third example in effect explains: Falstaff and reasons, that is rational explanations, will not keep company 'upon compulsion'. He cares little for principles of logic or literal truth. He is not foolish enough to believe that Hal will not notice how he inflates the number of his adversaries: it is a lie that is like himself, vast and still growing, and he relishes the elaboration of it. When he says 'I am a rogue if I drunk today' (l. 147) he pretends he is neither rogue nor drunk whereas he is of course unashamedly both. Even the discovery of his lies here does not discountenance him. 'A plain tale shall put you down' (l. 250) says the Prince, but of course it does no such thing and with an agility of wit that is such a contrast with his ponderousness of person Falstaff instantly creates a 'reason' which is as absurd as the lie which has been discovered. (The incident anticipates his later lies after the death of Hotspur.)

Yet his seemingly infinite inventiveness is not shapeless. His preposterous 'If . . . then' formulations are not the only repetitions. Falstaff relishes a fine phrase as he might a fine sherris-sack, and as with the wine, once is seldom enough. Notice how often he roars out the phrase with which he enters here, 'A plague of all cowards'. His moral pronouncements are rotund and frequently take the form of rhetorical questions like those we noticed in Hal's personification of his father: 'Is there no virtue extant?' (l. 115). Look too at lines 262–7 where he 'explains' his cowardice. Part of the irony here is there *is* an answer to these questions, and each time it is discomfiting.

Act III scene 1

If now you read again III.1 you may soon be aware not just of the immediate contrast in language with the previous scene but of contrasts and variations within the language of the new scene, just as there were in the previous tavern scene.

Re-read III.1 now, and make notes on the ways in which variations in idiom and language contribute to the thematic development of the play. You may still feel at this stage that though you can identify *where* there are significant variations, you cannot fully account for them. If so, simply mark those passages, and read on.

Perhaps the 'Welsh lady' (Mortimer's wife and Glendower's daughter) most vividly summarizes an important idea in the play here: that all the various kinds of differences between people are evident in the ways they speak. When we say of someone with whom we are at odds 'I don't speak his (or her) language' we are saying something which this play dramatizes.

This is a society riven by all kinds of divisions and in each quarrel the different factions do not speak the same language. (Conversely, the friendship between Hal and Falstaff is presented largely in terms of their being able to speak the same language.) The Welsh lady and her husband are not in fact at odds, but the awkwardness of their relationship underlines the hostility amongst the parties of the rebels, where Shakespeare shows far more antagonism being caused by differences of style and idiom than by more substantial differences. An historian attempting to compose an objective account of the disunity amongst the rebels would not emphasize this in their quarrel.

There is some contrast between the calm assurance of Mortimer's two opening lines and Hotspur's clumsiness and forgetfulness after it. But the contrast between Glendower's grandiloquence and Hotspur's plainness is far more vivid and important. Hotspur of course has been equally prone to be carried away by his own eloquence (see I.3.199 ff.) and here, finding himself outclassed, confines himself to the bluntness that is only half his character. Shakespeare reminds us that Hal's parody at II.4.100–7 was only half of Hotspur when here he gives Hotspur a speech as elaborate as Glendower's at line 22, 'O then the earth . . . '. At first you might find this confusing, for it is *not* of a piece with Hotspur's blunt

> Why, so it would have done
> At the same season if your mother's cat
> Had but kittened, though yourself had never been born. (ll. 15–17)

especially when you notice that Hotspur's rhetoric is a euphemistic way of saying that such upheavals in nature are as if the earth were breaking wind. But without it, we might forget how much Hotspur and Glendower are two of a kind. And later, when Hotspur complains that nothing sets his teeth on edge so much as 'mincing poetry' we might forget how much of the poet there is in him despite his protests. Hotspur and Glendower are as competitive in their grandiloquence as Falstaff and Hal are in mutual abuse. Indeed, Shakespeare seems to have introduced Glendower into his play solely for this competition, for neither Glendower nor his son-in-law take part in the Battle of Shrewsbury. It may help you define the tenor of Glendower's language if you read his part aloud and contrast it with the speeches of Mortimer and Worcester on page 102. The latter two are clipped and prosaic. Mortimer's similes ('valiant as a lion . . . as bountiful/As mines of India.') are commonplace, as are his colourless oaths ('In faith . . . faith he does'). There is not one inessential or unexpected adjective, nor any word that pleases by its unexpectedness. Worcester is a little more lordly, but equally stale. His lists of good and bad qualities come too pat to be interesting, and a word like 'haunting' (l. 180) seems under-employed. Hotspur's terse but good-humoured 'well, I am schooled' suggest he's heard it all before. Yet Mortimer and Worcester are speaking something much more like the reliable language of sound government than Glendower, who delights in declaring that his birth was signalled by disorder:

> The goats ran from the mountains, and the herds
> Were strangely clamorous to the frighted fields. (ll. 36–7)

The 'middling' language of Worcester and Mortimer throws Hotspur's plainness into relief too. Like many a person who claims to be blunt and makes truth his or her standard (see line 58), Hotspur is rude and aggressive. His humour is sometimes oafish (for example, lines 64–5). His antipathy to Glendower is temperamental rather than politic, something he 'cannot choose' (l. 142) though he can when he wishes put words together every bit as fluently as the Welsh magician:

> O, he is as tedious
> As a tired horse, a railing wife,
> Worse than a smoky house. I had rather live
> With cheese and garlic in a windmill, far,
> Than feed on cates and have him talk to me
> In any summer house in Christendom.

Glendower is all on one note. Hotspur, like Hal, is master of several voices: the fine breeziness of this passage is quite distinct from his sarcastic mimicry of Glendower's 'skimble-skamble stuff' at the beginning of the same speech.

It is a nice touch to make a song transform the quarrelling to temporary harmony once more. We can forget, when reading, that music was one of the many 'voices' that Shakespeare could command, and here it is as much a distinct tone as the intimate, silly, sexy banter between Hotspur and his wife. He is as disparaging about the song as he was about 'mincing poetry' but his unmistakable change of mood is a tacit acknowledgement of its power. II.4 began with Hal scrutinizing the language of the inn servants. This scene ends with Hotspur mimicking his wife's prissy oaths. Like Hal, he has a good ear. The two should have been brothers, not enemies. The likeness of the episodes that open the first of these scenes and conclude the other confirms how much of a pair the scenes are, and how much each complements the other. At the end of Act III Falstaff begins his concluding couplet 'Rare words! Brave world!'. After discovering how much of the play's meaning depends on various characters' consciousness of the words they use, we might take the phrase as a motto for the play: 'Rare words! Brave world!'

CPH

Acts IV and V

Let us now return to the final acts of *1 Henry IV*. We can regard them as forming a single movement or sequence, devoted to the Battle of Shrewsbury. A strange feeling runs through these battle-scenes: Shakespeare creates the impression of powerful and mysterious forces at work. It brings home to us what Graham Martin said in the Course Guide, that such a play is inconceivable without *verse*. When Vernon, in answer to Hotspur, describes Prince Hal as warrior (IV.1.97–110) we received a shock of enlargement and exaltation: it is as if Vernon were describing the morning of the world:

Vernon All furnished, all in arms,
All plumed like estridges that with the wind
Bated, like eagles having lately bathed,
Glittering in golden coats like images,
As full of spirit as the month of May,
And gorgeous as the sun at midsummer,
Wanton as youthful goats, wild as young bulls.
I saw young Harry with his beaver on,
His cuishes on his thighs, gallantly armed,
Rise from the ground like feathered Mercury,
And vaulted with such ease into his seat
As if an angel dropped down from the clouds
To turn and wind a fiery Pegasus,
And witch the world with noble horsemanship.

The point and force of these lines seems to derive partly from the unexpected link forged in them between the natural and the artificial. The artificial gear worn by Hal and his fellow knights, the ostrich plumes and glittering golden habergeons, are, in Vernon's eyes, so entirely the natural costume of that supremely natural activity, hand-to-hand combat, as to evoke the supreme and *superhuman* powers of Nature herself—above all, of the sun, the sovereign and source of all the world's living energies. Notice, too, how vivid is the contrast with the elderly and dispirited accents of the King, which are caught with equal mastery of character-drawing in the rhythms of:

How now, my Lord of Worcester! 'Tis not well
That you and I should meet upon such terms

As now we meet. You have deceived our trust,
And made us doff our easy robes of peace
To crush our old limbs in ungentle steel.
This is not well, my lord, this is not well.

(V.1.9–15)

That rueful phrase 'To crush our old limbs in ungentle steel' is strangely touching, I feel, and creates a sort of bond of physical fellowship between us and the stiff-jointed and despondent Henry.

Such effects as these would hardly have been attainable in prose. And more generally, we have here a demonstration of the resources of poetic drama. Had this been a play in realistic prose-dialogue, we should have expected somehow, even from Vernon's description, to be able to recognize the Prince Hal we know—the 'real' Hal, in a narrow sense of 'real'. Only in a poetic drama, perhaps (or, of course, in an opera), could we have the effect that Shakespeare is achieving here; that is to say, the removing of his drama to a new and altogether different plane of feeling, a plane on which Hal, and everything else, is for a moment transformed, so that we do *not* recognize them.

Evidently, in depicting a battle, a crucial concern for a dramatist must be to indicate how and when the outcome of the battle begins to reveal itself. Of course, in the present instance, the audience knows beforehand what the actual outcome will be, that is, that the rebels are defeated. What we are talking about, rather, is how and when the feeling that they will be defeated begins to communicate itself—to the participants, and to us the audience. Pretty plainly, it does so quite early on, in IV.1, when the news reaches the rebels that neither Northumberland nor Glendower will be joining them in the forthcoming battle, and that indeed they are most probably deserting the cause.

Will you now re-read this scene?

It is, surely, a remarkable and subtle scene. And in it the turning-point for the rebels' fortunes, it may be suggested, is not so much the bad news about their defecting allies as (and herein lies the subtlety) that memorable description by Vernon (the one we have just been discussing) of the newly-transformed Prince Hal. Hotspur senses at once that this is the news that counts most: 'No more, no more', he cries to Vernon. 'Worse than the sun in March/This praise doth nourish agues'. Why the news is so fatal can perhaps be explained thus: up to now it has been a strong card in the rebels' hand that chivalry and gallantry have seemed to lie on their side. The King's cause and motives are plainly dubious and to some degree sordid; and so perhaps are the rebels' also, if examined closely, but the rebels have on their side the heroic Douglas and the dazzling Hotspur—an indispensable advantage to their cause, for all that in the eyes of his father and uncle, Hotspur is a fool and a dangerous liability. Once, however, romance and gallantry—in the person of the metamorphosed Hal—become associated with the King's cause, the conviction arises in us, as it does in Vernon, that all is lost.

Vernon's role is curiously important. As regards the action he is an insignificant figure—nor is it very clear, if we bother to consider the matter, how he can have observed Prince Hal at such close quarters, in the midst of the enemy camp. Nor do we learn much about his character, save that he senses that he is on the wrong side but is too honourable to defect. But this unspoken appraisal of his, which is expressed again in V.2.51–9, when he enthusiastically describes Hal's chivalrous challenge to personal combat, influences us strongly and prepares us for the high emotion and chivalric ritual of Hotspur's destined defeat at Hal's hands.

If there is mastery in the subtle way that Shakespeare prepares us for this climax, what is equally masterly is the way he draws his themes to a knot in the final act. It is a bold and brilliant stroke immediately to follow Hal's noble funeral oration over Hotspur's body by his very different funeral oration over the shamming-dead Falstaff. It is one of the many devices, which also include most telling physical *tableaux*, by which Shakespeare makes us see further into that fundamental opposition: Falstaff versus Hotspur. It is an unresolvable philosophical opposition. Falstaff considers the supreme value to be Life ('Give me life, which if I can save, so' (V.3.59)). Hotspur considers it to be Honour and Glory, in comparison with which mere life is a trifle; and the two philosophies are presented with such powerful advocacy that they seem to us almost equally convincing.

Stephen Kemble as Falstaff, in Henry IV Part I, Covent Garden, 1802. (The Raymond Mander & Joe Mitchenson Theatre Collection)

What is striking, too, is that Falstaff is not, as you might vaguely have expected, diminished in this new atmosphere of heroism and chivalry, relapsing into mere 'comic relief'. On the contrary he grows more formidable. His sheer physical bulk, cunningly highlighted in the byplay with Hal (V.1.121–4), somehow reinforces this. In his great 'Honour' catechism (V.1.127–40)—'Can honour set to a leg? No. Or an arm? No . . . ' etc.—he is triumphantly persuasive and really quite hard to answer. And when he stabs the dead body of Hotspur, the dazzling exponent of Honour, and hoists the carcase on to his shoulder like some sportsman's prey, the deed has a foulness which makes him quite awesome.

An issue which has been much discussed, especially in a famous essay by the eighteenth-century critic Maurice Morgann, is whether Falstaff is to be considered a coward. In more recent times critics have tended, rightly, to frown on all such discussions that seem to imply that Shakespeare's characters are real flesh-and-blood people, about whom you can discover more than Shakespeare has chosen to tell us. Nevertheless I do not find this question about Falstaff absurd, and it leads on to some important considerations. Will you re-read pages 28–9 of P. H. Davison's Introduction, where he talks about Falstaff and Oldcastle? The historical Prince Hal came under the influence of the Wycliffite or 'Lollard' Oldcastle, who, though a brave man, was on religious grounds a *pacifist*. So what more natural than that Oldcastle should, in the folk-memory, have been transmuted into a *coward*? I imagine Shakespeare as assuming that his audience will expect Oldcastle/Falstaff to be a comic coward. However, he gives a direct hint that this is not the truth, when he makes Poins say (I.2.181–3) 'Well, for two of them [i.e. Bardolph and Peto], I know them to be as true-bred cowards as ever turned back, and for the third [Falstaff], if he fight longer than he sees reason, I'll forswear arms'. Thus, with considerable subtlety, he is presenting a Falstaff who is not something so obvious as a coward (after all, many of us are cowards), but rather a man who, on cogent philosophical grounds, rates self-preservation above all other values.

The point has a wider significance, for in *Hamlet* Shakespeare to my mind does something similar. He writes the play on the assumption that his audience, who will know the Hamlet story from earlier plays, expect Hamlet to be *mad*. It is thus a subtle and original stroke on his part to present a Hamlet who is merely *pretending* madness—a Hamlet, however, who is the victim of an acute emotional disorder. Again, and perhaps even more to the point, he writes a play which his audience knows to be a 'revenge tragedy', but he frustrates the expectations which this implies. What prevents Hamlet from immediately executing the vengeance prescribed by convention is not—we gradually come to perceive—mere practical difficulty, as in other 'revenge' plays, nor is it mere cowardice. It is, rather, doubts in Hamlet's mind about the duty of revenge and the nature of cowardice. Thus, the audience is compelled by the play to *re-evaluate* conventional categories and received ideas.

The Shakespeare I am trying to propose to you is a deeply *original* one, playing upon popular expectations but continually baffling and transcending them.

We have so far concerned ourselves with the leading characters in the play. Will you now turn your thoughts to certain of the minor characters, especially *Lady Percy*, *Mistress Quickly*, *Bardolph* and *Poins*, asking yourself how you would sum them up as individuals and in what ways Shakespeare is using them to further his designs? (This will entail some hunting back through the play.)

A word or two about *Mistress Quickly*. I should like to suggest that Shakespeare is making a charming and very sympathetic joke with regard to her. It is another example of his playing upon and defeating popular expectations. Mistress Quickly is presumably not only an inn-keeper but an ex-prostitute and, in a casual way, a brothel-keeper (see I.2.39–55). This at least is what we gather from hearsay, and what her name perhaps implies. However, when we meet her we find her an immensely respectable woman, full of professional dignity—a thoroughly nice and feeling woman, bewitched and ruthlessly exploited by Falstaff; and (this is the joke I am referring to) she is so innocent she is always innocently imagining bawdy allusions where none exists ('I am no thing to thank God on, I would thou shouldst know it'—III.3.117–18), or falling into bawdy *doubles entendres* without realizing she is doing so (' . . . thou or any man knows where to have me, thou knave, thou'). The joke is a humane and delicate one, very often ruined in stage-productions. As we shall see, Mistress Quickly, with a prostitute companion Doll Tearsheet, plays a larger part in *2 Henry IV* and the two women are the main representatives there of decency and good feeling. (It is Mistress Quickly who gives a very touching obituary of Falstaff in *Henry V*.)

Not everyone shares my view of Mistress Quickly, and I will quote a comment on what I have written from Professor Molly Mahood:

> Oh no! Not an *innocent* Mistress Quickly! It's surely not innocent to imagine bawdy where none exists: on the contrary!
>
> I am with you in finding Mistress Quickly a very likeable character. She can never say 'No', which is a kind of generosity, and this is Shakespeare's favourite virtue. So I agree absolutely that she must not be played as a hard-faced comic-postcard landlady. But if Shakespeare loves generosity, he is hard on duplicity—and Mistress Quickly, in her pretence of 'respectability', is continually and consciously deceptive. This makes her, for me, the reverse of innocent. Nearly all the laughs she raises are due to the audience's recognition that she is not what she wants to seem. Her social anxiety makes her see bawdy where none is intended; and I'm not sure it is mere simple-mindedness which makes her sound bawdy when she doesn't 'mean' to be—one could also give her choice of words a Freudian interpretation.

See which of these views you agree with, or whether you agree with either.

Now consider *Bardolph*; I suggest you assemble your impressions of him without help from me. Is he purely a foil for Falstaff's wit, or has he an individuality of his own and a positive function in the play?

Another point it would be worth asking yourself as you go back over the play is: is there any sign that, when writing it, Shakespeare was planning a sequel, or a possible sequel? John Purkis will be taking this point up in the next unit, but it would be an advantage for you to form an opinion on it beforehand.

PNF

Forum

Shakespeare and History

This section is meant to help with your work on *both* parts of *Henry IV*. It is intended to provide a background to the performance of the plays and to suggest why it was that Shakespeare chose to write history plays with this particular subject.

Its particular aim is to examine the relationship between Shakespeare's history plays, especially the *Henry IV* plays, and what people, at the time of their first performance, knew about the history of the fifteenth century. I will consider three aspects of this relationship.

(i) What people already knew about the reign of Henry IV as history.

(ii) What people already knew about the reign of Henry IV as drama.

(iii) The extent to which the plays portrayed scenes which had contemporary resonances for Elizabethan audiences.

(N.B. The spelling in all quotations has been modernized.)

Henry IV as History

In this section I shall examine what Elizabethan audiences knew of Henry IV's life and times. How familiar were the characters and events they saw portrayed? It is clear that Elizabethan audiences did know a certain amount about the reigns of Henry IV and Henry V. How did this come to be so?

It is easy for us to establish what plays were produced and what books were printed. We can also tell how many times plays were performed and how many books were printed and, therefore, roughly how many people might have seen a play or bought a book. From the content of a play or book we can also establish to some extent who the intended audience was. What we cannot tell is who *actually* saw plays and read books out of the population as a whole. We do not have evidence for making generalizations about mass audiences for plays or books. Most of the comments that are made about mass audiences are either inferred from the text of the play or book itself or its preface, or gathered from notes in contemporary letters and diaries. This kind of evidence is very scarce from the late sixteenth century; its availability does not increase until the later seventeenth century.

An additional problem is that it is almost impossible to arrive at an accurate estimate of what proportion of the population was literate. It is likely that the proportion increased in the late sixteenth and early seventeenth centuries because of the increase in educational provision and the growing importance of the written word. In a recent work on the subject (1982) Keith Wrightson says

> By the early seventeenth century the unlettered majority of the English population were everywhere faced in one degree or another with the applications of literacy and the products of a literate culture. It was a situation admirably symbolized by the fact that some of the traditional products of the oral culture had come to be disseminated primarily by means of the printed word.

Nevertheless, the attainment of literacy was strongly associated with the higher social classes and there were regional variations. Even in 1642, Dr Wrightson suggests, adult men overall were 70 per cent illiterate though illiteracy amongst the gentry had been virtually eradicated.*

In the 1590s when Shakespeare wrote the *Henry IV* plays there were numerous histories of England in print. These varied from the popular chronicles, like Edward Hall's *The Union of the Two Noble and Illustrious Families of Lancaster and York*, which was so well received that it went to five editions between 1542 and 1552, to the more scholarly and well-researched works of men like John Stowe, whose *Summary of English Chronicles* appeared in fourteen editions between 1565 and 1618. An edition was usually about 1200–1500 copies, but there was no copyright law and unauthorized editions and abridgements of popular works appeared in great numbers. Many writers, too, were fearless plagiarists of other people's work. These works of history seem to have varied in price from a few shillings to a couple of pounds. In 1611 Archbishop Ussher complained that an edition of John Speed's massive *History of Great Britain* was too expensive for him at three pounds. (It is almost impossible to give exact equivalents for present-day money values, but an income of £100 per annum was a substantial one and many poor clergymen lived on £20 per annum.)†

It is quite clear from the number of historical works published during Elizabeth's reign that they were an extremely popular form of reading matter. The most widely distributed works were chronicles and martyrologies. Chronicles were an ancient form of historical writing whose aim was to point the moral lesson of history. They drew on a literary and rhetorical tradition of writing to describe past events. However, the authors were influenced by the Renaissance interest in historical explanation and in discerning patterns and cycles in past events, but not to the same extent as the new school of more scholarly historians. Writers frequently drew only on earlier chronicles and regarded the production of new works primarily as commercial ventures. Martyrologies normally consisted of biographies of

*Wrightson, Keith (1982) *English Society, 1580–1680*, Hutchinson, pp. 195, 190.

†Wright, Lois B. (1965) *Middle Class Culture in Elizabethan England*, Cornell University Press, pp. 303, 308; Bennett, H. S. (1965) *English Books and Readers 1558–1603*, Cambridge University Press, p. 298; Sharpe, Kevin (1979) *Sir Robert Cotton 1586–1631*, Oxford University Press, p. 61.

Protestant martyrs and their precursors (Albigensians, for example) and descriptions of their martyrdoms. They gave the recently established Protestant Church of England a respectable historical pedigree. Both chronicles and martyrologies were strongly nationalistic.*

Why did people want to read chronicles? There is commonly an enhanced interest in the past, particularly in the details of a supposed golden age, when a nation has recently been through a period as traumatic as that of the Reformation. The reign of the Catholic Mary Tudor had then tried to reverse the Protestant Reformation, but Protestantism was re-established at Queen Elizabeth's accession. Certainly the authorities encouraged an interest in history. The City of London even established the office of city chronologer. Such history was safe and entertaining, but above all instructive. The chronicles provided a moral lesson, whether it was the evil of rebellion or the example of a fine ruler, and inspired patriotism, especially important in the 1580s and 90s with the problems of the succession and the threat from Spain. Furthermore, knowledge of English history, a subject not taught in schools and universities, was evidence of patriotism.†

The chronicles referred to here are those which were particularly influential, either because they formed the basis of other people's writing, or because they were very widely distributed. Polydore Virgil, an Italian Catholic, published his *History of England* in 1534. He wrote about English history from a Catholic viewpoint and was very unsympathetic to John Wycliffe and his followers, the Lollards. The Lollards were treated by their contemporaries in the fourteenth and fifteenth centuries as heretics, but many of their beliefs (rejecting transubstantiation, needing to make God's word in the Bible accessible in the vernacular, minimizing the role of the priest) were later adopted by Protestants. Virgil's chronicle was used by many later Protestant chroniclers, some of whom, nevertheless, were influenced by his hostility to a theology which could easily be seen as the forerunner of Protestantism.

Edward Hall, a lawyer, in his chronicle, *The Union of the Two Noble and Illustrious Families of Lancaster and York*, intended to improve upon Fabian's *Chronicle*, an earlier work based on Polydore Virgil. Hall sought to establish the respectable historical origins of the House of Tudor and the Church of England.

> In chronicles may be found that the most part of the ceremonies now used in the church of England were by princes either first invented, or at the least were established.

This was the first post-Reformation chronicle to glorify the Tudors and is perhaps one of the principal contributors to the 'Tudor myth', the myth that only the Tudor dynasty was keeping at bay the forces of disorder in English society. Hall took great liberties with his sources and invented most of the speeches which he put into the mouths of historical characters. He heightened the contrast between Prince Hal and Henry V by emphasizing the stories of Hal's riotous youth. It is not known whether these stories came from earlier, now lost, chronicles or whether Hall himself invented them. Hall's chronicle was itself extensively used by later chroniclers and his analysis of the fifteenth century certainly influenced Holinshed. There is some debate as to whether Shakespeare used Hall's chronicle for the *Henry IV* plays and you will find some discussion of this in the introduction to the New Penguin editions, *1 Henry IV*, pages 20–1, and *2 Henry IV*, pages 16–23 and 30–1.§

The next important chronicle was published in 1577. It was produced by a

*Burke, Peter (1969) *The Renaissance Sense of the Past*, Edward Arnold, pp. 2–3; Bennett, *op. cit.*, p. 215; Wright, *op. cit.*, pp. 304–7.

†Wright, *op. cit.*, p. 231.

§*Dictionary of National Biography*, Hall, Edward; McKisack, May (1971) *Mediaeval History in the Tudor Age*, Clarendon Press, pp. 107–10.

syndicate of London citizens, its 3000 pages having been compiled (rather than written) by Ralph Holinshed; a second edition was produced in 1587. It was primarily a commercial publishing venture whose aim was to make money for its backers. All three of the chronicles mentioned here, Virgil's, Hall's and Holinshed's, were further printed in unauthorized editions and abridgements, so they must have been more widely available than their publishing history would indicate.*

Martyrologies tried to do for the Protestant Church what chronicles did for the House of Tudor—to establish a respectable historical pedigree. Far and away the most important was John Foxe's *Acts and Monuments*, widely known as the *Book of Martyrs*. Most subsequent martyrologies were either abridgements of Foxe's immense work, over 2000 pages, or were largely based on it. Foxe began preparing the book while in exile on the continent during the reign of the Catholic Queen Mary Tudor. He was a close friend of John Bale, a fellow-exile and author of a chronicle of the Lollard knight Sir John Oldcastle (supposedly the original of Falstaff), who was presented as a Protestant martyr. Foxe's book reached its final form with the addition of the lives of the Marian martyrs, which Foxe wrote after his return to England on the accession of the Protestant Queen Elizabeth. In 1570 the government issued instructions that the second English edition, published that year, should be set up, with the Bible, for all to read in churches and other public places. *Acts and Monuments*, which, like the chronicles, appeared in many unauthorized forms, was the most widely distributed book after the Bible. It had overtly moral aims and fostered the idea, in a politically uneasy period, that the English were an 'elect nation', protected by God and guided by him to defend their faith.†

Foxe gives a highly selective account of English history, but it was very different from that of the chronicles. Foxe saw fifteenth-century English history in terms of Protestant heroes and Catholic villains whilst the chronicles portrayed it in terms of Henry IV's and Henry V's triumph over rebellion. We can illustrate this by comparing the chronicle accounts of Henry IV, Henry V and Sir John Oldcastle with those by Foxe. Holinshed wrote of Henry IV that

> In his latter days he showed himself so gentle, that he gat [*sic*] more love amongst the nobles and people of this realm, than he had purchased malice and evil in the beginning.

Yet Foxe saw him as

> the first of all English kings that began the unmerciful burning of Christ's saints for standing against the Pope

and goes on to say that

> such was the reign of this prince, that to the godly he was ever terrible, in his actions immeasureable, of few men heartily beloved; but princes never lack flatterers about them.§

Several chroniclers describe Prince Hal. Edward Hall said that he was

> turning insolency and wildness into gravity and soberness, and wavering vice into constant virtue.

*Wright, *op. cit.*, p. 314.

†Haller, William (1963) *Foxe's 'Book of Martyrs' and the Elect Nation*, Jonathan Cape, pp. 9–10, 55–8.

§Nicoll, A. and Nicoll, J. (eds.) (1978) *Holinshed's Chronicle as used in Shakespeare's Plays*, Everyman, p. 70; Foxe, John, *Acts and Monuments*, ed. Josiah Pratt, London, Religious Tract Society, vol. 3, p. 229, 4th edn. 1877.

Stowe gives us an interesting view of Hal's rejection of his youthful companions:

> to every one of whom he gave rich and bounteous gifts, and then commanded that as many as would change their manners as he intended to do, should abide with him in his court, and to all that would persevere in their former light conversation, he gave express commandment upon pain of their heads, never after that day to come into his presence.

Holinshed spared no compliments when Hal was transformed into King Henry V.

> This Henry was a king, of life without spot, a prince whom all men loved, and of none disdained, a captain against whom fortune never frowned, nor mischance once spurned, whose people him so severe a justicer both loved and obeyed (and so humane withall) that he left no offence unpunished, nor friendship unrewarded; a terror to rebels, and suppresser of sedition, his virtues notable, his qualities most praise-worthy.

Foxe is less scathing about Henry V than about Henry IV:

> seeing the memory of his worthy prowess, being sufficiently described in other writers in this our time, may both content the reader and unburden my labour herein

but he did say of him that

> This king, in his life and in all his doings, was so devout and serviceable to the pope and his chaplains that he was called of many the 'prince of priests'

—not in Foxe's view a praiseworthy description.*

It is important to understand that the view of English history presented by Foxe must have been at least as well known as anything from the chronicles. Foxe does not seem to have had much direct influence on Shakespeare's plays, but he was probably the single best-known writer on English history.

Falstaff/Oldcastle

You will recall from your reading so far that the character we know as Sir John Falstaff was originally named Sir John Oldcastle in Shakespeare's first draft of Part 1. Shakespeare probably adopted the name from an earlier play, *The Famous Victories of Henry V*, in which Sir John Oldcastle is shown as the companion of Henry V's youth. There was a historical character called Sir John Oldcastle who had been a close friend of Prince Henry's after they had fought together against Owen Glendower in 1400. Oldcastle then seems to have become involved with the Lollards and to have been seen as one of their leaders. He was an important figure because he was a gentleman and raised the movement above the status of popular heresy.†

The contrast between the chroniclers' and martyrologists' accounts of Oldcastle is even more marked than the contrast between their descriptions of the kings Henry IV and Henry V. Polydore Virgil was the main chronicle source for Oldcastle and provides the basis of the descriptions given by Hall and Holinshed, though Foxe reported that Hall used John Bale's (Protestant) account of Oldcastle's

*Hall, Edward (1550) *The Union of the Two Noble Families of Lancaster and York*, London, fol. (i); quoted in Bullough, G. (1966) *Narrative and Dramatic Sources of Shakespeare*, Routledge & Kegan Paul, vol. 4, p. 291; *Holinshed's Chronicle*, (1808) London, vol. 3, p. 133; Foxe, *op. cit.*, vol. 3, pp. 319, 579.

†McFarlane, K. B. (1972) *Wycliffe and English Nonconformity*, Penguin Books, pp. 145–6.

examination and death as well (*The Examination and Death of Sir John Oldcastle*, published in 1544). In fact Holinshed's account follows Hall's very closely: that about 1413 Oldcastle was accused of heresy by the Archbishop of Canterbury, Thomas Arundell. King Henry V appealed personally to Oldcastle who refused to abjure his beliefs, whereupon the king handed him back to the clergy. He was held in the Tower of London, examined by the archbishop, and pronounced a heretic. He escaped from the Tower and went into hiding. Meanwhile associates of his, led by another gentleman, Sir Robert Acton, attempted to co-ordinate a rebellion which was quickly suppressed by the king's men. Some of the rebels were hanged as traitors (K. B. McFarlane says thirty-one) and others hanged and burnt as heretics (McFarlane says seven). Hall concludes:

> some say that the occasion of their death was the conveyance of the Lord Cobham [Sir John Oldcastle] out of prison. Others write that it was both for treason and heresy as the record declareth. Certain affirm that it was feigned causes summarised by the spirituality more of displeasure than truth: the judgement whereof I leave to men indifferent.*

Although Hall is not prepared to make a historical judgement about Oldcastle, like other chroniclers he implicitly treats him as a man who is trying to upset the hard-won peace following the troubles of Richard II's reign. According to Hall, just as Henry IV established a settled regime, so Henry VII had established one under the House of Tudor, and those who threatened such regimes by rebellion, however worthy the cause, were to be condemned. Contrast this with the attitude of the martyrologists. Bale wrote that:

> Sir John Oldcastle died at the importune suit of the clergy, for calling upon a Christian reformation in that Romish church of theirs

and that not only was his martyrdom more worthy than Thomas à Becket's, but his hanging was equivalent to Christ's crucifixion. Foxe's account of Oldcastle was based closely on Bale's and was supplemented by his own research in Archbishop Arundell's registers. He also gave details of Oldcastle's beliefs, amongst the most important of which were his views on the papacy, of which Sir John said:

> as touching the pope and his spirituality, I owe them neither suit nor service, forasmuch as I know him, by the scriptures, to be the great Antichrist.

Having given his own account of Oldcastle, Foxe devotes forty pages to discussing how wrong the accounts in the chronicles were. He singles out for condemnation those of Virgil, Fabian and Hall because they treat Oldcastle as a traitor not as a heretic. The reason for Foxe's attitude is that, to a good Protestant, denying the Pope's authority may be heresy in the eyes of the Catholic church, but it is not a crime against the state. Foxe attacked the chroniclers for their pro-Catholic account of Oldcastle and the Lollards, whereas he saw the Lollards as forging the way ahead for the Reformation.†

As you can see, Elizabethan readers had two very different views of the reigns of Henry IV and Henry V. To the chroniclers Henry IV was the usurper king trying to make good his position. Oldcastle and the Lollards were a slight, but awkward, distraction from the main task of winning back the English lands in France which Henry V was to accomplish so gloriously. For Foxe, however, these reigns were periods of shameful persecution of true believers. The chroniclers

*Foxe, *op. cit.*, vol. 3, p. 377; McFarlane, *op. cit.*, p. 160; Hall, Edward (1809) *The Union of the Two Noble and Illustrious Families of Lancaster and York*, London, p. 49.
†Bale, John (1544) 'A brefe Chronycle concerning the examinacion and Death of the blessed Martir of Christ, Sir Johan Oldcastell the Lord Cobham', in *Harleian Miscellany*, vol. 2, 1809, pp. 278, 279; Foxe, *op. cit.*, vol. 3, pp. 322–3.

pointed to the lessons of statecraft, the need for a strong king, and the evils of rebellion. Foxe pointed to the evils of Roman Catholicism and of persecuting godly men.

Clearly Shakespeare's Sir John Oldcastle, renamed Sir John Falstaff, was not the same character as the chroniclers' rebel or as Bale's and Foxe's Protestant martyr. He may well have owed something to the real Hal's youthful companion at arms. It seems most likely that Shakespeare simply took over the character Sir John Oldcastle from *The Famous Victories of Henry V*. Oldcastle's descendants, the Cobham family, apparently complained about Shakespeare's portrayal of their ancestor, and Shakespeare changed the name to Falstaff. He had already used the name as Sir John Fastolf in *1 Henry VI*, a man thought by Hall and Holinshed to be a Lollard and who was certainly accused of military cowardice. However this man was born two years after Henry V's accession. Another Sir John Fastolf of Norfolk was sued by Sir John Oldcastle's father-in-law and there was a brawl in court for which Fastolf was bound over to keep the peace. It seems far more likely, however, that Shakespeare's use of these names derives from a mixture of memory and imagination than that they were faithfully drawn from real historical characters.*

Some writers have considered that Falstaff's frequent references to the Scriptures show that Shakespeare intended him to be seen as a Lollard. Others, including P. H. Davidson, have argued that Falstaff is an anti-Puritan satire. Most Puritans were members of the Church of England who wanted minor reforms because they felt that the Reformation had not gone far enough. A very small minority, better called separatists than Puritans, established radical Protestant self-governing congregations independent of the established church. Foreign observers, commenting upon Puritanism, did not distinguish between its different shades. It was the separatists who were satirized, for example, in Ben Jonson's play of 1614 *Bartholomew Fair*. These separatists were considerably fewer in number and less influential in the late sixteenth century than they became in the early seventeenth century, though the government certainly regarded them as a threat to political stability, just as Henry IV and Henry V had seen the Lollards.

It is easy to exaggerate the extent to which Puritans were mocked in sixteenth-century drama. A reference such as that which Falstaff makes in *1 Henry IV*, I.2.94 to 'the wicked', which the editor describes in the notes as 'current Puritan jargon', gives a false Puritan emphasis to a belief which was widespread amongst most English Protestants, both radical and conservative. The majority of Anglicans in the late sixteenth century believed in predestination, damnation, and the importance of preaching the word. Falstaff's attitude is less anti-Puritan than anti-clerical. He is part of a popular tradition of scoffing. References such as those he makes to repenting and psalm-singing (*1 Henry IV*, III.3.4–9, II.4.129) are made in a spirit of mocking all religion rather than of mocking Puritanism alone.† It is difficult, if you take this view, to see any connection between the historical Sir John Oldcastle and Shakespeare's Falstaff, except to say that they were both insubordinate to established authority.

Henry IV as Drama

Is has been suggested that as well as the anonymous play *The Famous Victories of Henry V* of about 1586–8, there were also several other plays about Henry IV and Henry V which have not survived. A. R. Humphreys believes that *The Famous Victories* was originally written in two parts and that the first part was performed in a non-extant version which so familiarized Elizabethan audiences with Oldcastle

*Bullough, *op. cit.*, vol. 3, pp. 171–2.

†*1 Henry IV* (New Penguin Shakespeare) p. 31 and see such examples as the commentary on *1 Henry IV*, I.2. 82–7 and 94, and *2 Henry IV*, I.2.36–7; McGrath, Patrick (1967) *Papists and Puritans under Elizabeth I*, Blandford, pp. 304–13, 353; Collinson, Patrick (1967) *The Elizabethan Puritan Movement*, Jonathan Cape, pp. 359, 432–47; Hill, Christopher (1966) *Society and Puritanism in Pre-Revolutionary England*, Mercury Books, pp. 16–17.

that Shakespeare took their familiarity for granted. There is, however, no evidence to show how many times *The Famous Victories* was performed, nor for how well known it was to the audiences of Shakespeare's plays. Hall's *Chronicle* seems to have been the principal source for the *Famous Victories*. It certainly reflects the same emphasis—wild young Hal, noble conquering Henry V. The play owes nothing to the historical tradition of John Foxe, even though Hal's fat drinking companion is called Sir John Oldcastle. In fact Foxe was an important source for a number of biographical plays. There is evidence to suppose that Shakespeare used him for *Henry VIII*. The first part of the *True and honourable History of the Life of Sir John Oldcastle, the Good Lord Cobham* was written in 1599 by Munday, Drayton, Wilson and Hathaway, apparently at the request of the Cobham family, to counteract the disrespectful portrayal of Falstaff/Oldcastle in Shakespeare's plays. ('It is no pamper'd glutton we present'.) It appears to be based on Foxe's view of Oldcastle. In the same year, John Weaver wrote *The Mirror for Martyrs* in which he clears Oldcastle of any connection with the rising which bears his name, but which was led by Sir Robert Acton. The importance of the *Famous Victories* lies in its being the earliest surviving history or chronicle play of the type that became particularly important after the Armada (1588). In a rash of nationalist fervour many history plays appeared, all owing far more to chronicle accounts of English kingship than to Protestant history. Indeed they followed an increasingly outdated view of English history as the work of scholarly historians like Stow superseded the work of the chroniclers.*

Henry IV and the 1590s

It is almost impossible to calculate the extent to which Elizabethan audiences saw allusions to contemporary events in the two *Henry IV* plays. There are various kinds of reference which it might have been possible for them to see: to specific events, to activities common to both the early fifteenth century and the late sixteenth century, and to moods or atmospheres common to both periods.

The moral that rebellion is wrong, deriving from the chronicles, is clearly apparent in both parts of *Henry IV*. However, it is very unlikely that this was intended to refer directly to the most serious rebellion of Elizabeth's reign, the rising of the Northern earls in 1569, an attempt to secure the release of Mary Stuart (Queen of Scots) from imprisonment and to recognize her as heir-presumptive to the English throne. It was not a Catholic plot that would have benefited English Catholics in the long term. The rebellion had only limited support and was badly led, so it was quickly suppressed. It is most improbable that Shakespeare was referring directly to a rising which had taken place nearly thirty years earlier. Much more significant was the general fear of rebellion in the 1580s and 90s. During the 1580s there were several plots involving Mary Stuart and English Roman Catholics. Mary's execution in 1587 was crucial in Philip II of Spain's decision to invade England in 1588. Two further attempted invasions took place in the 1590s and Tyrone's rebellion, which spread through the whole of Ireland between 1594 and 1598, received Spanish aid. Coupled with concern over the succession, for no one was certain that James VI of Scotland would be allowed to assume the throne peacefully on Elizabeth's death, these threats aroused serious concern over the country's stability, both internal and external. Many of Elizabeth's subjects must have felt themselves to be living in a society similar to that ruled over by Henry IV and Henry V in which peace and stability were hard won and by no means certain for the future.

This general feeling of insecurity gives the theme of rumour in the second part of the *Henry IV* plays a greater force. Rumour, as a character, was a traditional presence in plays and the subject of rumour had a particular relevance for the rumour-ridden 1590s. It is clear that the most serious threat posed by the Catholic

*Bullough, *op. cit.*, vol. 3, p. 159; *1 Henry IV*, Arden Edition, Humphreys, A. R. (ed.) Methuen, 6th edn. 1978, p. xxxvi; Ribner, Irving (1965) *The English History Play in the Age of Shakespeare*, Methuen, pp. 200–3.

plots was the fear that they aroused rather than the actual risk they posed to political stability and the Protestant succession. Another source of alarm was the anonymous Marprelate tracts, published between 1588 and 1589, savagely attacking the bishops. These caused the authorities far more anxiety than was warranted by the subversion of the tracts themselves. Only two years after the Star Chamber decree on printing, which established a licensing system for printers and publications, the author of the Marprelate tracts was able to evade discovery, even after the printers had been unveiled and examined under torture.

Another subject which had both general and specific applications for sixteenth-century audiences was recruiting. It was an activity common to both the early fifteenth century and the late sixteenth century, though there may have been little similarity in the way in which it was done. The Elizabethan militia, for example, was not required to serve outside the county in which it was raised. Such similarity as there is may well have been exaggerated. Lindsay Boynton writes in *The Elizabethan Militia* that Sir John Fortescue's classic *History of the British Army*, published in 1899,

> seriously referred his readers to Shakespeare for further information, and followed his own advice by writing an account [of Tudor armies] based largely on the history plays.

So those commentators on the recruiting scene in *2 Henry IV* who sought further information on recruiting practices in the fifteenth century from Fortescue's nineteenth-century history, would find themselves directed back to Shakespeare. There is at least one recent work on Elizabeth's military forces which quotes the recruiting scene in *2 Henry IV* as its evidence.*

Certainly the abuses in raising soldiers portrayed in *2 Henry IV* were familiar to sixteenth-century audiences; abuses for which both the Justices of the Peace and the captains were blamed. The Privy Council complained that Justices in Dorset had recruited two men to serve as captains who had no experience of war—one was too old and the other too given to books and study. Some JPs levied more men than necessary and pocketed the recruitment money. Others conscripted rogues and vagabonds, revoking sentences they had received for criminal activities. Captains were involved in financial rackets concerning arms and equipment—sometimes with the connivance of the county military authorities—and in defrauding soldiers of their pay.†

It is difficult to know whether the view of Henry IV, the usurper who brought stability, and Henry V, the patriot who won such a glorious victory over the French, were seen to have any direct contemporary relevance. There was the very loose analogy that the Tudors had brought stability out of chaos and Elizabeth had defeated Spain, but it was unlikely that such imprecise associations had much force in the *Henry IV* plays compared with the more immediate messages they imparted.

Conclusion

I have tried to suggest what Elizabethan audiences would recognize when they went to see Shakespeare's *Henry IV* plays. I have also tried to show that Shakespeare drew upon only one of the two historical traditions with which his audience would have been familiar. He chose the heroic chronicle history, which was also a long-standing stage tradition, rather than the Protestant martyrology history, although there was a school of plays based on this as well. We cannot be certain of what detailed references to contemporary events audiences of Shakespeare's plays would recognize, but we can guess at the general references they might have made and it is the scope of these that I have tried to demonstrate. *AL*

*Boynton, Lindsay (1967) *The Elizabethan Militia*, Routledge & Kegan Paul, p. 5; Cruickshank, C. G. (1966) *Elizabeth's Army*, Clarendon Press, 2nd edn. p. 22.
†Cruickshank, *op. cit.*, pp. 21, 27; Boynton, *op. cit.*, pp. 168–9.

Henry IV

Part 2

Prepared for the Course Team by John Purkis

What happens in Henry IV Part Two

Fluellen It is not well done, mark you now to take the tales out of my mouth ere it is made and finished. I speak but in the figures and comparisons of it; as Alexander kill'd his friend Cleitus, being in his ales and his cups, so also Harry Monmouth, being in his right wits and his good judgements, turn'd away the fat knight with the great belly doublet; he was full of jests, and gipes, and knaveries, and mocks; I have forgot his name.
Gower Sir John Falstaff.
Fluellen That is he. I'll tell you there is good men porn at Monmouth.

(*Henry V*, IV.7.43–55)

IN this section I propose to work quickly through the action of the play, and then, in subsequent sections, discuss some leading ideas in isolation. As a caution, though, first of all, remember the words of your editor P. H. Davison: '*2 Henry IV* presents more problems for the producer and the reader than any other of Shakespeare's history plays. It will not respond to simple and single-minded approaches' (set text, page 39). Even as we unpick the fabric of the play, we must not lose sight of its controlled complexity. In order to help you sort out what is going on, I have to make use of the acts and scenes into which your text is divided. It is conventional and convenient to use these divisions, but two points should be borne in mind. First, as Nick Furbank has already explained, the standard act and scene-divisions in many of Shakespeare's plays, including this one, are first supplied in the First Folio text of 1623; many Elizabethan plays don't make use of these divisions, which breaks up the flow of the action. Secondly, you should note that the scene divisions in Act IV are supplied by *later* editors, and that in P. H. Davison's edition a compromise has been arrived at: the text is allowed to flow as if there were only two scenes in Act IV, but the traditional lineation is kept for purposes of reference (see page 163 and the headnotes mentioned there).

Look again at the King's last speech in *1 Henry IV* both to remind yourself of 'the story' and also to see it as 'pointing forward' rather than 'concluding the action'.

Now read the 'Induction' to *2 Henry IV* (p. 51).

Was there anything like this in *1 Henry IV*? What exactly is gained by the presence of Rumour?

No, everything in *1 Henry IV* was presented dramatically, not narrated in this way. This is the first inconsistency between the two parts of *Henry IV*; later you will see that the *2 Henry IV* has an Epilogue as well.

Rumour, as a character, is an echo of classical epic and tragedy. It alludes to Virgil's *fama* or 'fame' (*Aeneid* IV, 173–88) and to the personified figures used by Seneca in his tragedies. These were frequently imitated by the Elizabethans, for example the character of Revenge in Kyd's *The Spanish Tragedy*. The presence of such a character is perhaps a signal to the reader or spectator that we are entering a world tonally different from *1 Henry IV*.

A producer could make Rumour look like the apparition of a god, with a frightening mask or clothing (see I.1 'painted full of tongues'). But on a simpler level, of course, he/she is there to provide a recapitulation of the story so far, and to point to ambiguities in what is to come—'small comforts false, worse than true wrongs'. (See P. H. Davison's note on page 167 of the set text.)

Act I

Now read on to the end of I.1, at first paying most attention to the story. As well as using the editor's notes, make your own notes so that you have a summary of the action of the scene to help you when you return to the play later.

What is the emotional movement within the mind of Northumberland and how does it reach its climax? What happens in the last section (after line 161)?

As Rumour prophesied, Northumberland is presented first with 'smooth comforts false', though you could hardly say that he is convinced by them, and then the facts begin to emerge. He keeps his control, believes the worst (line 81), and is not particularly reassured by line 82: 'Douglas is living and your brother yet'. His agitation is evidently increasing from lines 83 to 103; finally the long narrative by Morton provokes an equally long reaction from Northumberland (lines 136–60) in which he lets go and abandons all restraint. It is difficult, as your editor's note suggests, to estimate the effect of this speech on an Elizabethan audience. We are told that 'Let Order die' (line 154) would have been an unthinkable and horrifying notion, implying that the whole universe was coming apart. Remember this speech and compare it with the 'mad' speeches of King Lear, which you will encounter in Block VI.

The last section reverses the movement and a kind of normality (for rebels!) begins to reassert itself. Northumberland has gone too far in his 'passion' (lines 161 and 165), and the two other characters persuade him into positive action. One might note that such 'persuasion-speeches' are a characteristic feature of the history plays, and not only the history plays, but in Shakespeare's work generally. The audience seems to have responded to scenes in which a character, determined to follow a course of action—or, as in this case, depressed to the point of inaction, is *persuaded* by another character to reverse, or at any rate to change his or her attitude to, the action at first proposed. Make a note of this, and look out for other examples of 'persuasion-speeches.'

Now read on to the end of Act I, making notes as before.

Notice that Falstaff has been 'severed' (I.2.205) from the Prince, though their preceding adventures are alluded to: 'Gad's Hill' (line 151) and 'Shrewsbury' (lines 61 and 150). The introduction of the Lord Chief Justice in this first Falstaff scene is important. Though Falstaff cheeks him, he has previously 'sent for' Falstaff (line 101)—the charges against Falstaff are still on the books (lines 60–1 and 150). *Did you notice the constant references to 'age' and 'death' and 'sickness'?* We will take this up later. The fact that the King is rumoured to have had an 'apoplexy' (line 108) indicates that a crisis in affairs of state may be imminent.

The meeting of the rebels in I.3 should advance our interest in their cause. They are determined to revenge the death of Richard II and allege that they have popular support (lines 101–7). But the *mood* of the scene is depressing and overcast with premonitions of gloom.

Though we shall not go into detail at this stage, *did you notice the frequent references to the text of the Bible in both scenes?* If not, check the editor's notes again.

Act II

Now read on to the end of Act II, making use of the editor's notes. Here are four short questions which are intended to give you a sense of direction.

(1) How are the interests and ideas in I.3 pursued and developed through Act II?

(2) Look at the Hostess's famous accusation against Falstaff (II.1.83–101). It is not easy to write about humour, but have you any comment about this passage? Can you see any Bible references here? What exactly is their function?

(3) Can you suggest any particular reason why Pistol—a new character, remember—would have been amusing to an Elizabethan audience?

(4) What is the point, in the general setting of Act II, of the verse scene 3?

---

(1) Generally, Falstaff's world is established and enlarged upon, but the ideas of law and justice are immediately reintroduced. In II.1.1, the word 'action' brings in the law. Falstaff is to be called to account for his debt to the Hostess. The Lord Chief Justice returns in line 60. Although Falstaff is able to talk his way round the Hostess and is able to get her to advance him even more money for his 'consumption of the purse' (I.2.238–9), the greater account remains to be paid at a later date:

> *Doll* . . . when wilt thou leave fighting a-days, and foining a-nights, and begin to patch up thine old body for heaven?
> *Falstaff* Peace, good Doll, do not speak like a death's-head; do not bid me remember mine end.
>
> (II.4.227–30)

At the very end of Act II the society of the tavern is dispersed by the threat of war.

(2) The first way to appreciate the prose in the passage is to read it aloud. The rhythms are specific to the Hostess; the other characters have their own way of using prose—look at Falstaff's and the Lord Chief Justice's speeches further down for comparison. The Hostess's constant departures from the point at issue have their own use to her: they authenticate the place and time in a ludicrous way, and one can imagine that they are based upon listening to a real person.

You will not find the references to the Bible in the notes, and should turn to accounts of Holy Week (not 'Wheeson week') in the Gospels, in particular the Last Supper, to get the point. Luke 22 is one starting point; use the Authorized Version (though this post-dates our text it retains the language of earlier versions).

The points of comparison are minute in themselves, but seem to add up. The scene is an upper room (the goodwife 'goes downstairs'). Much is made of the 'goblet'—the cup or chalice—and the 'dish' appears later. The 'washing' of the 'wound' can refer to Jesus's wounds, but also to the 'washing' of the disciples' feet. There are two references each to 'swearing' and 'denial' which echo the repeated denial of Christ by Peter. 'Vinegar' is offered to Christ during the Crucifixion. Christ 'desired to eat' the Passover feast with his disciples, and promised that each of them would later be given a kingdom—'ere long they should call me madam'. Finally, and surely more convincingly, consider the sentence.

> 'And didst thou not kiss me, and bid me fetch thee thirty shillings?'

bringing in the kiss with which Judas betrayed Jesus, and the thirty pieces of silver.

The Hostess is not conscious of what she is doing, but if she were a real person, we might say that the idea of *betrayal* has started up a chain of free associations in her mind. These are elaborated into a *parody* of the Gospel narrative. What Shakespeare is doing is more to the point; he has made a connection between Falstaff and Judas which is simultaneously humorous—they are not alike, are they?—and deadly: perhaps Falstaff is not just a funny fellow, but much more wicked than we realize (in the Middle Ages Judas was the greatest villain in human history).

This example of minute analysis enables us to appreciate the density of reference in a passage of Shakespeare (and there are obviously many other references in that passage besides those discussed). In *King Lear* the speeches of Poor Tom, the Fool, and the mad King will make this exercise on the Hostess's accusation seem like child's play.

(3) See pages 213–16. This is rather an unfair question if you are totally unfamiliar with Elizabethan literature. Briefly, Pistol is a walking parody of the diction used in Christopher Marlowe's *Tamburlaine the Great*, and similar bombastic (ranting) plays. (Shakespeare was himself accused of bombast by Ben Jonson.) I think it is important to see Shakespeare using previous *literature*, as well as *observation* (the Hostess), in creating humorous characters.

(4) It keeps the main action of the play in mind, and prepares us for the defection of Northumberland. As your editor remarks (p. 36) this little scene is frequently cut, but it serves to remind us of what we have lost. Do you agree with this?

Act III

Now read III.1, and also listen to the performance on cassette 5 (P). Do you have any comments on the scene, considering that the play is called *Henry IV*? How would you describe the King's condition? What happens in this scene?

This is the first time that the King has appeared on stage in this play. Though there have been rumours about his health, we now see for ourselves:

(i) That he is in his nightgown, as opposed to a kingly costume.

(ii) That he has been very ill and his recovery seems in some doubt (lines 100–2).

(iii) That he can't sleep (lines 1–31).

(iv) That the past and the dethroning of Richard II seem more vividly present to his mind than the need for action against the rebels—compare the long reminiscence (lines 45–75) to the much shorter speech at lines 88–92. You could refer to guilt and 'Nemesis' (unavoidable retribution).

Though you could say that nothing much happens in this scene, and that it hardly advances the action of the play, it is in fact a strange, almost haunting, scene and repays close examination. I would suggest that the main speeches are (a) longer than is strictly necessary, and (b) picked out from the main body of the text by their copious imagery and elevated tone. At this exalted level Shakespeare may use the 'poetry' to inculcate general or 'moral' observations, whose truth extends beyond the play. The poetic language helps to reinforce this intention.

Let us try to test these generalizations. Please re-read the whole scene, and then return to lines 4–31. Is this speech essential to the action? Comment on the speech in the light of the preceding discussion.

Well, is the speech necessary? You could substitute line 3

> . . . Make good speed.
>
> *Exit page, King attempts to sleep. Enter Warwick and Surrey.*

but I suppose it might seem slightly ridiculous to have the King 'attempting to sleep' at all, and you could begin the scene with

> *King apparently asleep in his nightgown. To him enter Warwick and Surrey.*
>
> *Warwick* Many good morrows to your majesty!

What we would lose, at the simplest level, is the King's preoccupation with the responsibilities of kingship, and his insights into the life of his 'poorest subjects'. These insights extend beyond the play—while not suggesting that they are out of context—into generalizations about sleep and kingship which finally crystallize into the proverbial 'Uneasy lies the head that wears a crown'. This expression, as Donald Davie has pointed out, has 'gone into the store of folk-wisdom'.*

The 'realistic' way in which the speech reflects the preoccupations of a sleepless person might well be commented on. The 'dozing off' leads the mind into constructing dream-pictures, which, in the vision of the sea, intensify into a nightmare; this in its turn jerks the sleeper back into full consciousness with the word 'awakes'. Syntax 'mimes' the mental process, because the long sentences are all *questions*—admittedly of rhetorical and circular nature—which leave the problem 'hanging' and unresolved. Only at the end of the speech is there a *statement*, which caps or seals off what has gone before. At this point the poor King might have at last dropped off, but business re-enters with Warwick and Surrey.

Finally, though, we can tie the speech into the action of the play: this king cannot sleep because he is a usurper. As your commentary points out, the idea of the good unsleeping king is taken up in *Henry V*, IV.1, but elsewhere Shakespeare constantly associates sleeplessness with guilt. Just as the famous 'Sleep no more' passages in *Macbeth* are the result of the murder of Duncan, so it could be argued that King Henry is punished in this way for the deposition and death of Richard II.

Now read III.2. Here we move to Gloucestershire (see headnote to III.2 on page 228). How would you play the scene down to line 51? How does your attitude to Falstaff change as the scene continues?

There are many ways of playing this scene, and P. H. Davison hints at this before coming down on one side, when he suggests that it represents 'kindly humour and warm humanity'. Notice the allegorical names for the Justices; you may have suggested that they are to be gulled because they are witless country people. The mood is one of reminiscence ('Do you remember?'); the scene is also shot through with references to Death and the dead. (You may have noticed that a similar mood returns at line 190.)

The recruiting sequence might be said to show us how Falstaff can corrupt even the gentle country folk, who might be compared to the mechanicals of *A Midsummer Night's Dream*, until we realise that it is Bullcalf and Mouldy who begin the bribery. Falstaff is not unwilling to take the bribes, and this diminishes him in our eyes; his final speech, announcing his intention to deceive the justices to his own advantage, is distinctly unpleasant. See Davison's comment on lines 298–301 in which it is suggested that this prepares the 'audience for the rejection of Falstaff'.

Act IV

Act IV is the central act. In it Northumberland pulls out of the battle, the rebels are defeated and the crisis of the King's health is finally resolved—he is about to die, but the merits of the Prince of Wales are now clear. *You will find the exercises on this act included in the section on the language of the play.*

* For a full discussion of this point see Davie, Donald (1955) *Articulate Energy: An Enquiry into the Syntax of English Poetry*, Routledge and Kegan Paul, chapter V. Davie deals with several sixteenth and seventeenth-century passages on the theme of sleep, and compares them to the King's speech in *2 Henry IV*.

In addition, I suggest you spend some time considering the character of Prince John as revealed in his speeches and what view you take of his treatment of the rebels. Compare Falstaff's acceptance of the surrender of Coleville and John's subsequent actions: is Falstaff out of place here? And if so, do you still think badly of him? I leave you to answer these questions if you have time.

IV.5 will be examined in the second television programme and discussed in the Broadcast Notes; meanwhile consider the function of the 'persuasion-speeches' (see p. 44): the *action* is within them. Notice how the Prince, in his meditation by the bedside of his father (IV.5.25–9) takes up the theme of 'Uneasy lies the head that wears a crown' from the speech in Act III which we have already looked at. *JP*

The Language of the Play

Gaultree Forest

I want now to look at IV.1 and 2. The prospect of such long stretches of blank verse, apportioned between a number of apparently indistinguishable nobles (as here), or Romans, or lords and gentlemen of the court (as happens in other plays) can be very daunting to the reader. So I want now to suggest some guidance that may help you to discover the dramatic structure of scenes like this, and to see how the longer speeches are put together. *Please re-read these scenes now.* You could try marking off the rebels' speeches in one colour, and those of the King's party in another; further, give each member of the two factions a different sign—say a cross for the Archbishop, an asterisk for Mowbray and a dot for Hastings. This may seem pointless, but can you tell Hastings from Mowbray without it? Read each one as the actor who has been allocated the part must do and you will see that they are not a double act, not merely supporters of the Archbishop indiscriminately supplied with fragments of the story that Shakespeare wants to tell. Look, for example, at Mowbray's first three speeches: a mere four and a half lines altogether.

What information has the Archbishop communicated in lines 5–16? What is his tone? And how would you characterize Mowbray's response? Five lines later, how does he react to the messenger's news? And is his next line (l. 26) anything more than exposition for the audience's sake?

Old Northumberland (Hotspur's father—see I.1 and II.3) has let them down. The Archbishop announces this grave news in dry, and understated, terms: 'Their *cold* intent'; 'The which he could not levy'; perhaps the phrase 'retired to ripe' is the most pungent expression of his bitterness. In contrast, Mowbray's energetic metaphor expresses catastrophic disintegration. And yet the next time he speaks, so soon afterwards, he expresses first satisfaction, that the enemy's strength had been so accurately assessed, and second, eagerness to be up and at them. As for 'I think it is my lord of Westmorland;' that 'think' could suggest he does not know Westmorland very well but expository functions tend to be allocated to the less important speakers. We have seen however, that Mowbray has already been given the basis of a 'character', cues from which the actor can create a distinctive, and in this case volatile, presence. We can even see that Hastings, in the same passage, is not a mere mechanical part, but a *contrasting presence.* A character whose speech we are not reading tends to disappear from the mind's unreliable stage; but on the real stage, the actor is still there—and still acting.

Between lines 29 and 96 the Archbishop and Westmorland *make representation* of their differences. I put it like that because quite clearly Shakespeare is not attempting a realistic reconstruction of what happened at Gaultree Forest. Each 'opens' with a long speech. I suggest you look again at Graham Martin's analysis of the King's speech from *1 Henry IV*, III.2.60–84, in the Course Guide. That speech is, frankly, something of a bravura piece, the difficult thing made to seem effortless. The surface elaboration all depends on a very simply syntactical structure. These speeches are not as elaborate, but they are complicated enough for the reader, or the actor, to lose the thread. Westmorland's scornful characterization of rebellion (as it looks to one secure in power) can seem like a glimpse of the landscape before the fog closes in. But when we looked at the speech which opens the first play we saw how firm its basic syntax is. And here too the kind of words that seem hardly worth noticing because they have no kind of poetic energy will repay attention: in particular, the conjunctions, and the conjoining phrases, which Shakespeare habitually used with special care. The 'if' which begins Westmorland's sentence at line 32 is emphatically repeated at the beginning of line 36 ('I say, if . . . ') and followed by what at first seems to be a more literal version of what was so graphically expressed after the first 'if'. Read lines 32–6 again. Westmorland is claiming that the 'true, native', and most popular shape of 'damned commotion', or rebellion, is always what he claims it to be in the disparaging tones of the first part of the sentence:

> . . . base and abject routs,
> Led on by bloody youth, guarded with rage,
> And countenanced by boys and beggary.

(For a good example of a textual dilemma, look at the note on the phrase 'guarded with rage' on pages 241–2.) Westmorland's argument is orthodox, but not watertight. The very possibility of a justified rebellion was an issue that Shakespeare had to handle very delicately. Westmorland is diplomatically suggesting that if the Archbishop really knew what rebellion is, he would not be supporting it. Those two 'ifs' are completed by the subjunctive forms of the verbs 'appeared' and 'Had not been'. (They have nothing to do with the past tense.) Westmorland is pretending to believe that for an Archbishop to be in rebellion is a logical impossibility, and so his second sentence (l. 41) is a question: why has every attribute of the Archbishop that is associated with peace been 'ill translated' into war? In line 47 the word 'wherefore' tells us that this question is a kind of hinge, and all that precedes it is turned round after it. You can literally *see* how orderly the first part of the sentence is. Four successive lines begin with 'whose' and in five lines the word 'peace' occurs four times, the only line without it helping to build up its impact in the fifth line. The very orderliness of the words enhances Westmorland's implied contention that peace and order are the same. Look at the prepositions in the second part of the sentence (after 'wherefore') and you can see how carefully it is still controlled: 'Out of . . . Into . . . ' and 'to' four times. The stability of peace has been turned *into* the headlong movement of war. The sentence has an architecture of its own.

Now read the Archbishop's reply (ll. 53–87) and even if you feel you have grasped it perfectly, identify the words and phrases Shakespeare uses to indicate each movement and stage of the Archbishop's argument.

Each new point is carefully signalled: 'But' (l. 59), 'Nor' (l. 61) and 'But' (l. 63) are all emphatically at the beginnings of lines. (Shakespeare had no silly qualms about beginning sentences with conjunctions.) More elaborately at line 66 the Archbishop says 'Hear me more plainly', and surely it is true that what follows *is* plainer, and is succinctly expressed in lines such as 'And find our griefs heavier than our offences' (l. 69) and in lines 73–9.

I am not going to deplore the fact that grammar is no longer taught, but there are certain fundamental principles of grammar that can help you become a more adept reader if you are conscious of them. I have already drawn your attention to the way conjunctions act as signals, and in *1 Henry IV* as well as here we have occasion to notice that where there is an 'if' a 'then' or its equivalent will follow (or the other way round). It seems too obvious to mention that every subject will usually have a verb, and that verbs may have objects. But look at the sentence which begins at line 80 'The dangers of the days but newly gone'. It consists of so many clauses that you may well get lost—as in fact I think Shakespeare did. But identify the subject's main verb, and thus isolate the main clause, and the hub of the sentence will stand out clearly:

> The dangers of the days but newly gone . . . . (l. 80)
> Hath put us in these ill beseeming arms . . . (l. 84)

There are many occasions on which you have to wait even longer for a main verb. It's a question of confidence. At first you may want a sentence to make sense too quickly. How can you cope with so many variations and subordinate clauses before you reach the safety of the verb on which so much depends? You can, with practice. It's so easy to forget that Shakespeare's sentences were written to be spoken by actors who know how those sentences will fall out and how they end.

'This fellow doth not stand upon points' says Theseus in *A Midsummer Night's Dream* of an amateur actor who ignores all punctuation. Points, and in particular full stops, must be fully registered. Each complete sentence is a distinct unit. Modern editors are often responsible for lesser punctuation, but most of the stops are indicated in the earliest printed texts and mark the actor's voice breaks. Observing them will help to reveal how a long speech is organized.

All this may seem very mechanical, but I believe it would be pointless to draw your attention to, say, the Archbishop's references to disease and to time if we had left entirely to chance your ability to follow the argument of a lengthy passage of blank verse.

Next I want to draw your attention to an aspect of the dramatic construction of this scene. So far all that we have heard about war has been very abstract, and very polite. But now the pace changes. You can *see* (on p. 115) a group of shorter speeches.

Read lines 88–104 and think about their effect on the stage.

Professor Molly Mahood points out that Westmorland is trying to drive a wedge between the Archbishop and the two other rebels here. In Westmorland's first speech words with connotations of dress, such as 'guarded' (l. 34), 'shape' (l. 37), 'dress' (l. 35), and 'investments' (l. 45) suggest, in Professor Mahood's words, that the Archbishop is not

> really part of the insurrection, but just the rebels' front man . . .
> The Archbishop makes a dignified and trenchant reply in which the image of a disease in the body politic shows how deeply he feels himself to be committed.

She goes on to point out that in this quicker exchange (ll. 88–104) the ploy is repeated far more blatantly. Look at Westmorland's repetition of 'your' and 'you'—always in a different, but stressed position within the line. The text tells the actor how to say it.

But the Archbishop refuses to be set apart (ll. 93–4). And Westmorland tries yet again:

> There is no need of any such redress,
> Or if there were, it not belongs to you.

It is at this moment that Mowbray joins the argument (perhaps he literally joins the Archbishop too), and Westmorland, changing tack, turns to address *his* particular grievances.

Read from Mowbray's 'Why not to him' (l. 97) down to 'more than the King' at line 138 and make a note of all the references to time.

The word that chimes through these lines is 'then', and sometimes 'when'. Mowbray's description of the climactic moment when history might have been changed if Richard II had allowed Mowbray's father to fight Bolingbroke in the lists (see note on line 123, page 245) is introduced 'Then, then, when'. Look again to see how such words point up the structure of the speeches. Of course it would be distinctly 'ham' for an actor to stress each 'then' too heavily, but the modulations of the voice can be used to suggest the fatal differences between then and now. The passing of time is not just stressed in this play to give a pleasing depth to the picture.

But so much talk of 'then' makes Westmorland impatient again. And if you read on you can see that again the tension mounts to a barefaced revelation of Westmorland's arrogance (at lines 158–9) and this time it is the milder mannered Hastings who steps in. But his attempt to change the subject does nothing to defuse Westmorland's anger, 'I muse you make so slight a question' (l. 165), and the Archbishop returns to the fray. It is three against one, but there is no doubt which side is stronger: the rebels spend the time Westmorland is off stage trying to reassure one another.

There is really no scene change at this point (see note p. 248). There is neither space nor need for me to investigate IV.2 as thoroughly as the previous scene. But read it carefully because it completes the episode, and you will need to know what happens. The note on lines 54–65 suggests that an Elizabethan audience would have viewed Prince John's treachery in a better light than we do, and that by associating this trick with the King's son instead of solely with Westmorland (as Holinshed does) Shakespeare was enhancing the authority of the Royal House. But surely Prince John is a very chilling figure? Look at his rebuke to Hastings at lines 50–1, and at the speech which ends the scene. What is the effect of the change to rhyme at line 118? Doesn't it give everything in the last six lines the jaded air of cliché? See the note on line 121, page 251.

Now read IV.3 and make notes on how it reflects on what has happened in the two previous scenes.

After a long and sober episode the sudden eruption of Falstaff on to the stage is very welcome, not just because we know the mood will lighten, but because he is warm, human and fallible (and despicable), whereas Prince John and Westmorland are ruthless, chilling and efficient (and admirable). Falstaff makes the constrast explicit at the beginning of his long speech at line 85. But there is a more precise comment on the events of the previous scenes in lines 64–9. Coleville is bitter because his leaders were not 'won . . . dearer'—that is, defeated at a higher cost to the King's party. Falstaff's implication that the whole party may have given themselves away 'gratis' not only disparages the rebels, but undermines the honour of Prince John, who had so solemnly promised to redress the Archbishop's grievances (IV.2.114–16). Davison points out (pp. 252–3) that this scene parallels that with Hotspur in *1 Henry IV*, V.4 for it was then that Falstaff propounded the idea that all notions of honour between enemies are futile. The urge to survive knows nothing of the discriminations of honour, and Falstaff's presence in this coda to the Gaultree Forest episode challenges the deadly formality of the previous scenes. Shakespeare got the idea of the ceremonial drink to cement the false bargain from Holinshed. In the 1982 RSC production there was an extraordinary moment when Westmorland expressionlessly, and of course wordlessly, put away the glasses before (in mid-sentence) turning to the arrests. The cynical misuse of ceremonial drinking is counter-balanced in this scene by Falstaff's tribute to the genial virtues of 'A good sherris-sack'. But Falstaff is by now an unreliable spokesman for the virtues we call 'humanity'. We examine this question more closely when we look at the three 'Gloucestershire' scenes together.

The Gloucestershire Scenes

Re-read III.2 and V.1 and 3.

Look at III.2.1–80 and comment on the effects produced by the use of proper names in the passage, on the references to time and death, and on any references to language itself which remind you of work we did on *1 Henry IV*.

After the preceding scene ('Uneasy lies the head that wears the crown') we are suddenly in a more commonplace, familiar and even more populous world. It is a world that has its points of contact with the great world of historical events: John of Gaunt (Henry IV's father) is familiarly mentioned (l. 43). (Falstaff thinks Shallow is showing off (line 293 ff.).) So is Thomas Mowbray, father to the rebellious Mowbray in this play and then Falstaff's master! But these great names take their place amongst the friends of Shallow's youth. The place names too, homely though they be, evoke the quintessence of both town (Gray's Inn) and country (Stamford fair). 'Jesu, Jesu, the mad days that I have spent!' says Shallow, and laments with his friend Silence the certainty of death and the toll it has taken of all their friends. Why Shallow is so named is explained by the opening of Falstaff's last speech (line 291: and IV.2.50–5 suggests another, more cryptic answer). But do we agree with Falstaff's appraisal? (Read the whole speech.) Although Shallow skims lightly from the contemplation of morality to the price of bullocks (l. 37) or ewes (l. 47) his lively refusal to live entirely on memories makes him as profoundly worthy of our respect as the more sententious broodings of those loftier characters who cannot come to terms with the disappointment of their expectations.

John Purkis shows (page 66) how both Hal and Falstaff seem to have lost some of their vitality in this play. But the loss in them is partly revealed and partly made good by two small parts: Bardolph and Pistol. They are difficult to read, but both are plums for actors. Shallow's interest in the new word Bardolph uses is of a piece with his interest in fatstock prices. And Davison's rather drab note (among so many that are very illuminating) fails to take account of the pleasure Shakespeare took in the mutability of language. His own use of language was of course prodigiously inventive; but he would also send up affectations of speech such as this high-falutin latinism. Bardolph relishes the sound of it, though he has no idea of what it means. In *1 Henry IV*, II.4 we saw how Hal in particular was specially conscious of the varieties of language about him. (And compare Doll Tearsheet's comment on the way in which 'occupy' has changed its meaning at II.4.144.) Davison suggests (note to lines 298–301) that seeing Shallow's 'hospitality so abused goes a little way to prepare an audience for the rejection of Falstaff'. Before proceeding be sure you are fully aware of what other elements in this scene are to Falstaff's discredit. I am certain that by the end of the play he is more to be wondered at than loved, but whether all his faults actually make the rejection of him more palatable (I am not talking about expediency: he clearly has to go) is, as John Purkis will stress, a question you should be able to explore, if not to answer. We *ought* by the end of this scene to know that Falstaff is a monster. He has abused his commission. Remember his 'ragamuffins' in *1 Henry IV*: 'There's not three of my hundred-and-fifty left alive—and they are for the town's end, to beg during life' (V.3.36–8). Now, because they do not offer a bribe Feeble and Shadow are for death or the town's end. But Shakespeare clearly did not want to paint Falstaff's conduct here all black. First, there's the spirit in which Feeble belies his name. Second, why should he give to a character he meant us to despise the wonderful line 'We have heard the chimes at midnight, Master Shallow' (the effect is incomplete without the name), combining nostalgia with grandiloquence to strike a note that is elegiac without being lugubrious.

Turn now to V.1. The opening supplies a good example of a joke that we hardly notice on the page but which should be hilarious on the stage. A character, here Shallow, gets stuck on a perfectly ordinary word—here, 'excuse'. He uses it so many times that the word comes to seem funny in itself. (For another example look at Mistress Quickly and 'swagger' II.4.71–105.)

Though so much briefer, and without any equivalent of Falstaff's corrupt recruiting methods, the scene is similar in construction to the earlier Gloucestershire scene: an episode involving Shallow and his little world is then cynically glossed by Falstaff in a manner that is half astute and yet half increases our liking for silly Shallow. Look at Davison's excellent note on line 58. The social cohesion which Falstaff disparages as rustic *naïveté* ('Their spirits are so married in conjunction, with the participation of society, that they flock together in consent, like so many wild geese') is once again partially expressed in terms of the characters' responsiveness to language. I keep repeating this point because it not only makes explicit Shakespeare's own consciousness of language (which we in any case could hardly fail to miss) but vividly suggests that he could rely on his audience sharing this consciousness, even if not to so highly developed a degree. Here Shallow congratulates Davy on his awful pun (lines 29–31: a 'conceit' is a fanciful trick of language) thus encouraging his servant in a whole sequence of plays on Visor (the name of his less-than-honest friend and also used colloquially for 'face' because that is what a visor covers) and 'countenance'. The serious point behind the joke is that a pleasure in words may obscure the moral issue involved. Fine words often do put butter on parsnips.

V.3 is a virtuoso piece. Read it, listen to it on the cassette and/or follow it in the text whilst listening to it.

It is always risky to use metaphors from other arts to try to define literary effects. Nevertheless I think it is useful to think of the different 'voices' Shakespeare could command as if they were instruments in an orchestra, each striking a different note and capable of almost infinite combinations. And this is a scene in which several notes chime happily together.

Will you now identify the different voices and try to define what each one contributes to the mood of the scene. What note or flavour, to begin at the beginning, is introduced by Shallow's first speech? (Don't forget to make use of your editor's notes.)

Shallow's orchard, his arbour, his pippins and his caraways suggest rural tranquillity, hospitality, generosity and good fellowship. His leisurely repetitions show that drink has made him even more mellow. Bardolph is (at first) uncharacteristically silent—has drink made him morose?—it could be funny on the stage; but Silence on the other hand is unstoppable. He finds a cue for a jovial song in everything, even though his more natural disposition is as he so unforgettably describes it at line 38. Falstaff, it's worth noting, does not dominate the group *verbally*, which is unusual for him. Davy is up and down with food and drink and chat and though the page, 'my little tiny thief' (l. 56), has nothing to say, his size and his youth will make an eloquent contrast with at least four of the group. But with an effect as dramatic as a shot (hence, surely, his name) in bursts Pistol, with the news from London. Davison's note describes the variations in his bombast, and you should look at Pistol's part in II.4.106–202 where the threat of his 'swaggering' so much agitates Mistress Quickly (see above). Remember also how Falstaff exercised himself briefly in a similar vein in *1 Henry IV*, II.4.379–89, where Mistress Quickly says 'he doth it as like one of these harlotry players as ever I see!'

Of course the real significance of the impact of Pistol's news is its dramatic irony—the effect, that is, which comes from us knowing much more than the people on stage know. For genial and exuberant though this scene is, we miss much of its effect by taking it out of context. If you failed to appreciate this point, re-read the scene that precedes it to see how ill-founded Falstaff's confidence really is. But I am not altogether convinced by Davison's note on lines 134–6. Might not an Elizabethan audience have been sophisticated enough to relish a thought of the kind of anarchy Falstaff represents even while they were sensible enough to know that it would never do? And if we postulate an audience appalled by Falstaff's levity, grimly muttering 'that proves it, he'll have to go', then are we to imagine that same audience applauding the display of law and order that follows in V.4? Are we to imagine that Shakespeare meant such a scene to be applauded? You might pause to consider the fact that V.4 has often been left out of stage productions.

CPH

Act V

WE return from the detailed study included in 'The Language of the Play' to a quick résumé of the final act of the play. The important point to notice is the way in which the main story—the death of Henry IV and the accession of Henry V—breaks into the peace of the Gloucestershire countryside; that interruption is appropriately Pistol's function. Falstaff intends to trick Shallow and at the same time has become a monster of self-delusion.

What is the main point of V.2 and V.4? Is the ending of the play (V.5) unexpected?

V.2 We do not know how the Lord Chief Justice will be received (he is also being restored to the play—he has been off-stage since II.1). The new King, after a mock show of offence, embraces both the person and the allegorical virtue of Justice: notice the constant reference to the Justice as 'father' in the last speech. Henry V makes his peace with 'the patriarchy', and the effect is seen in V.4.

V.4 In this little scene the world surrounding our usual picture of Falstaff and Hal—the life of the tavern and the bawdy house—is destroyed before us as the women are led away. It is also apparent what the nastier side of that 'jolly' world is; it has led to violence and murder: 'The man is dead that you and Pistol beat amongst you' (ll. 16–17). The scene helps to prepare us for V.5.

V.5 All roads have led to this finale. Though it appears short in length it contains two processions, which would have been dressed magnificently, and would have taken up a good deal of stage time. This symbolically represents Hal's transformation. Falstaff, Pistol and Shallow line up on one side of the stage, reminding us of the Eastcheap Tavern and the Gloucestershire episodes. Doll's incarceration is also mentioned (l. 33). After the procession returns from the coronation, their over-zealous protestations of loyalty are rebuked. Aristotle said that a recognition scene is intensely dramatic. (By a 'recognition scene' I mean a scene in which a character is brought to see that another character is a long lost friend or relative whose identity had been concealed from him or her.)

This is a recognition scene in which the expected recognition does *not* take place—'I know thee not, old man' (l. 50). The true natures of Hal and Falstaff are shown to be incompatible: 'being awaked I do despise my dream' (l. 54). Falstaff, because of his delusions, is unable to accept what is happening to him, and continues to believe that 'I shall be sent for' (l. 92), but it is the Lord Chief Justice with whom these words were first associated in I.2.101. The entry of the Justice *with Prince John* indicates that a more severe punishment is in store for Falstaff than the banishment decreed by the King; the disorderly company associated with Falstaff is sent to the Fleet Prison, and the civil and military authorities are left occupying the stage. Though their last words are extremely moderate in tone, Prince John's prophecy of a war with France takes up the old King's last words to his son

> busy giddy minds
> With foreign quarrels (IV.5.213–4)

In fact, there is very little in the last scene that is not already prepared for in the earlier scenes of the play.

The promise of Falstaff's return by the speaker of the Epilogue remains a problem which Davison deals with very copiously (pages 285–6): if the plays from *Richard II* to *Henry V* are taken in sequence, then there is really no place for the values represented by Falstaff (for example, his views on honour) in the militarism of the final play. In fact the Epilogue only promises that Falstaff will 'die of a sweat', which is roughly what happens in the next play. Falstaff does not reappear in *Henry V* but dies off-stage. You will find the scene from *Henry V* at the end of cassette 5 (P), side A.

The Rejection of Falstaff

'Oh, don't die, dear master!' answered Sancho in tears. 'Take my advice and live many years. For the maddest thing a man can do in this life is to let himself die just like that, without anybody killing him, but just finished off by his own melancholy.'

('The Death of Don Quixote' from Cervantes, *Don Quixote*)*

IN this section I want to call your attention to a matter which has always exercised the spectators and the readers of this play. In order to prepare yourself read V.5 again and P. H. Davison's Introduction, pages 31–9; remind yourself too of the Falstaff of *1 Henry IV* by reading Davison's Introduction to that play, page 16 on Morality Plays, page 25 on Falstaff's 'wit', and pages 30–1 in praise of Falstaff. Then consider these questions:

(1) Why is Falstaff's rejection unavoidable?

(2) What does this rejection mean?

(3) Why might some people find it difficult or impossible to accept the rejection?

---

(1) In answering the question you should begin by treating Falstaff as a character within a play. The play is a written text, a constructed and enclosed dramatic world. Falstaff is rejected in the same way that the 'sweet prince' in *Hamlet* is killed: in both cases an ending to the play is required, and has been prepared for. If you find this answer unsatisfactory, then let us move on to the next question.

(2) The meaning of rejection is hardly obscure especially if you accept the view that the *Henry IV* plays are Morality Plays about the education of a Prince. Prince Hal eventually matures and becomes Henry V, and, like the central character in a Morality Play, rejects Vice (Falstaff) and embraces the kingly virtue of justice (the Lord Chief Justice). Even if you don't like this final stage of Hal/Henry V's character and find his militarism odious, it is still possible to explain the meaning of the rejection by 'reversing the terms'. Shakespeare, you might then say, shows the conqueror of France deciding to strip himself of 'common humanity' (Falstaff) before going into battle. You may have noticed that Davison finds this view too simple and his argument has as its climax: 'Humanity is *not* rejected with Falstaff' (page 39). Nevertheless, the 'common humanity' aspects of Falstaff are very appealing and cannot be ruled out of court.

(3) Let us develop this further, and try to consider the third question, why some people find it difficult to accept the rejection at all. Almost the first words Falstaff addresses to Prince Hal are: 'Shall there be gallows standing in England when thou art king?' (*1 Henry IV*, 1.2.58–9). Although it is somewhat premature in our history to see this as an enlightened plea for the abolition of capital punishment, the drift of Falstaff's argument is towards the opposite of the severity represented by the law and the Lord Chief Justice. In the playlet contained in *1 Henry IV*, II.4, Falstaff is crowned with a cushion: as Maurice Hussey has pointed out

> On the stage the effect can be uproarious and serious at the same time. If we glance at the symbolic meaning of the cushion that he places on his head to suit his words we shall understand him. A cushion, iconographically, is a symbol for lenience and mercy . . .
>
> (*The World of Shakespeare and his Contemporaries*, p. 84)

* Cervantes, *Don Quixote*, Penguin edn. (1950), p. 937.

Hal, one might argue, tricks Falstaff into loving him: Falstaff becomes a substitute for his own real, dreary and guilt-ridden father; but Prince Henry has always kept us aware that he is only using Falstaff as a kind of cover:

> I know you all, and will awhile uphold
> The unyoked humour of your idleness.
> Yet herein will I imitate the sun,
> Who doth permit the base contagious clouds
> To smother up his beauty from the world . . .
>
> (*1 Henry IV*, I.2.193–7)

Taken literally this is almost too nasty; but even if we concede that Hal is giving information about his character for the benefit of the audience because this was an Elizabethan stage convention, the general idea remains unpleasant. Hal is grooming himself for his place in the patriarchal power structure by flirting with low life but forming no permanent relationships there. You could say that Hal *uses* people, he does not love them, and love is one way of describing Falstaff's relation to Hal. Hal only simulates enjoyment of Falstaff's world, and is *really* all the time on the side of justice and death. Those gallows are not going to come down.

Of course, *Hal's* rejection of what he has never come to terms with, understood or valued is not therefore what is distressing, if you accept this account of him. What is alarming is the implied statement of the whole play, that Shakespeare as author *shares* Hal's attitude and wishes us the audience to participate in the rejection. This is what gives offence, and provokes the audience to respond actively, demanding Falstaff's resurrection to placate an attack on the deeper generosities of our being.

Against all this rather wet sentimentality one could make one final tough-minded point, once again 'reversing the terms', that Falstaff is never defeated, and that in the two plays taken together, his 'world' has 'stolen the show'. His section of the text—the sub-plot—has undermined and subverted the official play of *Henry IV* which it was only intended to counterpoint. Nobody has ever asked to see the character of Henry IV again, but Queen Elizabeth I demanded to see another play about Falstaff. Falstaff wins out in the end.

In fact, to change the subject slightly, but I think relevantly, the way in which characters like Falstaff or Hamlet, or, to take non-Shakespearean examples, Don Juan and Don Quixote,* continue to live on beyond and outside their texts is a permanent affront to that school of criticism which believes that literature only exists 'on the page' or as a manifestation of language alone. Such characters attract moral, metaphysical and speculative discussion, and may be regarded as psychological archetypes; to rule out such discussion as 'mistaken' or 'illegitimate' will not prevent people from indulging in it. In making this point about Falstaff in particular, I would not wish to extend it to all of Shakespeare's characters; even quite major figures like King Lear or Othello, for example, seem to me to be firmly locked in their plays, perhaps because those plays provide them with appropriate channels for their potentialities which are then, as it were, exhausted. Coleridge posited a Hamlet who never found a world of action suitable to his talents; similarly we might feel that there is more to be said about Falstaff: he is full of unexploited *capabilities*. It is interesting that when the theatres were closed in the middle of the seventeenth century, it was Falstaff and his cronies who survived through the commonwealth in a farce called *The Bouncing Knight*.

* The contemporaneity of Don Quixote and Sir John, their 'texts' both appearing at the beginning of the seventeenth century, may well represent desire throughout Europe to have done with the honorific survivals of feudalism.

Frontispiece to Francis Kirkman The Wits . . . , *1671. Reproduced by permission of The British Library Board.*

One of our earliest Shakespearean critics, Margaret Cavendish, Duchess of Newcastle (1624–74), in praising Shakespeare, ventured to enquire: 'Who would not think he had been such a man as his Sir John Falstaff?' And in the next century Dr Johnson was moved to exclaim in his edition of Shakespeare: 'But Falstaff unimitated, inimitable Falstaff, how shall I describe thee?' In 1777 the high point of this school of criticism was reached when Maurice Morgann published

An Essay on the Dramatic Character of Sir John Falstaff, claiming that the knight had been sadly misunderstood.

> The ideas which I have formed concerning the Courage and Military Character of the Dramatic Sir John Falstaff, are so different from those which I find generally to prevail in the world, that I shall take the liberty of stating my sentiments on the subject; in the hope that some person as unengaged as myself, will either correct and reform my error in this respect; or, joining himself to my opinion, redeem me from, what I may call, the reproach of singularity.

To sum up, the rejection of Falstaff may be a dramatic necessity but the values Falstaff stands for remain undefeated. The playwright has created a supremely intelligent and subversive being, who, like the jinnee of eastern legends, cannot be 'bottled up' inside the confines of a 'text'. To invent such a character is given to very few authors indeed, and is one of the reasons that we acknowledge the supreme ability of Shakespeare.

Imagery and themes: some optional exercises

Themes, Madam—nay, it is: I know not Themes.

(Kenneth Tynan, replying to an American lady who asked him to explain the themes in *Hamlet*.)

TYNAN was right, of course. There is no alternative to engaging with the play itself. Nevertheless, I would be failing in my duty if I didn't indicate, at this early stage in the course, another way of working at a Shakespearean text which developed into a critical method in the middle of this century. If you regard the text as a dramatic poem, it seems reasonable to try to read it *as a poem*, and to pick out chains of imagery or major themes in the text; the first book to develop this method extensively—*Shakespeare's Imagery* by Caroline Spurgeon—was concerned to elucidate, among other things, what the method revealed about Shakespeare the man. At a more useful level, the method encouraged us to see Shakespeare developing his interests in certain topics from play to play; *2 Henry VI* is not, for example, the only play about the problems of kingship, usurpation and the succession, and it might be useful in reading *Hamlet* to compare Claudius's situation with Henry IV's and to see how some of Hal's princely qualities are re-expressed in young Hamlet.

The following exercises are meant to help you to develop this way of reading *into* and *beneath* the text of the play.

The Archbishop's speech in IV.1.53–87 is already familiar to you. What imagery does it contain in lines 54–67? Now look back for examples of the same imagery to I.1.137–47 and I.2.1–5, 93–132, 180–7 and 238–51. Then turn to III.1.38–44.

References to *disease* are common in this play, both at a literal level, and in the imagery. Northumberland and Falstaff are examples of two prominent characters who, at their first entries in Act I, are pointed out as sick men.

Northumberland (I.1.137–47) is traditionally played 'in his night gown' as befits a sick person who should be in bed; and in his speech he also refers ('as a wretch . . . ') to a more extreme/manic form of sickness to describe his condition.

Falstaff has sent his urine for analysis (I.2.1–5); in the later part of the scene he refers to the sickness of the Lord Chief Justice (l. 95), to that of the King (ll. 103–8), to Galen, author of the standard medical text (l. 118), and makes jokes about 'deafness', 'disease', 'potions', etc. Yet it is the Lord Chief Justice who sees Falstaff as visibly decrepit, admittedly from age as much as anything (ll. 180–7). Finally, Falstaff hobbles off, afflicted with gout, but in addition joking about the 'disease' which afflicts his purse (ll. 238–51).

Now look at III.1.38–44 for an extension of the idea to 'the body of the kingdom', spoken by the sick king. The comparison is, in one sense, almost a cliché, but it has become ominous, like a theme in a piece of music that becomes obsessive by constant repetition. And so the Archbishop's speech, coming at a stage when the continuing sickness of the King must now determine the fortunes of the state, also extends the imagery to the nation as a whole: 'we are all diseased' (IV.1.54), and this has been caused by excessive eating and drinking; the standard medieval treatments of 'bleeding' (l. 47), 'dieting' (l. 64) and 'purging' (l. 65) are to be administered by the acts of rebellion and war.

On this model, using both literal examples as well as comparisons, make lists of references

(1) to age, ageing and old people

(2) to time, and the passing of time

in *2 Henry IV*, and write a commentary on them.

It has been frequently observed that there is a preponderance of *old people* in this play and that associated references to *age* and the *passing of time* are common. (You will have found that there is a close connection with the theme of *disease* already mentioned, and also, though it is not an illness, with *lack of sleep or rest.*) For some examples, look at Davison's Introduction (pp. 35–7) and consider his views on 'this accumulation of aged persons'.

Remembering how Rumour prefaced the play and referred to 'false reports' and 'smooth comforts false, worse than true wrongs', make a list of major examples of 'deceits' and 'ambiguous' happenings in the play; ignore those in the very first scene, to which Rumour is obviously referring. Can you find any metaphor or imagery which reflects this mood of doubt?

In this play it is Northumberland who will once again display 'craft' in holding back his troops from the rebellion; on the other side Prince John's 'most Christian care' in capturing his opponents by a trick (IV.2) surely cannot be dismissed as the approved way of dealing with rebels to whom no promise need be kept. The 'false death' of King Henry IV leads Prince Hal to assume the crown prematurely, and Hal is shown to be fully prepared to disown his comrades in a most calculating way: 'the noble change that I have purposed' (IV.5.155). Falstaff, too, has deceived Mistress Quickly and is full of plans to trick Shallow out of his money.

Imagery is more difficult to bring into the list, but consider

> As with the tide swelled up unto his height
> That makes a still-stand, running neither way. (II.3.63–4)

or some of the comparisons on page 119, in particular

> He cannot so precisely weed this land
> As his misdoubts present occasion.
> His foes are so enrooted with his friends
> That, plucking to unfix an enemy,
> He doth unfasten so and shake a friend. (IV.1.203–7)

(You'll meet 'the unweeded garden' again in *Hamlet.*)

Now, from a quite different point of view, what do you consider was the political theme of the play which would have most interested the Elizabethan audience? The play was first printed in 1600.

Hanging over the society of the play, and therefore of England, is the threatened death of the old King; people were uncertain what to expect from the heir. The 'transfer of power', as we would call it, was particularly full of contemporary meaning to an Elizabethan audience, for everybody knew, in the late 1590s, that Elizabeth I had not long to live. She was the last of her line, the original heir—Mary Queen of Scots—had been put to death, and James's succession had not yet been confirmed. Even if it was to be James, he was resident in a far away country and unknown to the English. The clear statement of the new king

> This is the English, not the Turkish court;
> Not Amurath an Amurath succeeds, [who killed his brothers]
> But Harry Harry . . . (V.2.47–9)

was surely meant to provide reassurance to the audience.

What is the official 'message' of the play concerning the cure of the country's ills? What abstract quality is regarded as the great positive virtue?

Justice is stressed, in both the stories within the play, as the overriding virtue which will purge the land of guilt and ensure that the transfer of power happens smoothly. Rebellion is to be dealt with by summary justice—I may have been too sentimental in discussing Prince John on page 63. Notice that the Lord Chief Justice is called by his title, not his name; in the folk tale, he imprisoned the heir to the throne for striking him (this is mentioned at I.2.53–4 though not dramatized in either play). By keeping to his title he presents an *allegorical* contrast to Falstaff who may be regarded as the figure of Vice: Falstaff's power is limited but he is easily able to corrupt the country Justice, Shallow. Falstaff's plans depend upon Hal's succession, and the fears of the Lord Chief Justice and the King's brothers are very real. They can imagine Falstaff 'in power', the Falstaff who says 'the laws of England are at my commandment' (V.3.134–5). Falstaff is also set against the Lord Chief Justice in another way: he and his cronies are off-duty military figures (notice the addition of Pistol to the cast in this play); the barbarity of the soldiery, which may be appropriate on a battlefield, is out of place on the streets of London—the Lord Chief Justice represents the civil power. The unrestrained license of the wayward soldiery—and by extension that of the provincial warlords who plague England with rebellion—is brought to an end when the new King Henry chooses to *reinstate* the Lord Chief Justice.

Is this the only answer? What other scenes of the play contain positive values?

The Gloucestershire scenes. Read carefully the end of Davison's Introduction, pages 37–9, and again listen to V.3 on cassette 5 (P). Davison's rich account of the 'character' called *England* is very persuasive: just as Rupert Brooke put as many Cambridgeshire place-names as he could into 'The Old Vicarage, Grantchester', so that the poem works like an incantation, so Shakespeare seems, almost unnecessarily, to provide a roll-call of country names, and includes a countryman's reminiscences of a *past* London, which was itself a country town where everybody seemed to know each other. The purpose of all this, according to Davison (p. 39), is to re-establish values which seem to have disappeared from the grimmer parts of the play, including Falstaff's *present* London, and to guarantee that in the end 'England' will win through. (You must judge this argument on its merits, and may forgive yourself if you did not notice all this when first reading the play!)

The unity of 1 Henry IV and 2 Henry IV

How did any *one* of the following differ from any one of the other?
(1) Henry IV Part I
(2) Henry IV Part II

(Exam question from *1066 and All That*)

THAT the second part of *Henry IV* was composed after the first part has never (yet) been disputed; beyond that, however, all is speculation. You will find, at the one extreme, those who insist that *Henry IV* is a single unitary text, divided, like Christopher Marlowe's *Tamburlaine the Great*, into two parts because it was impossible to stage it otherwise in the time available; at the other extreme, *Part Two* has been regarded as an unplanned afterthought, a completely separate play, and finally, as an independent work which contains entirely new characters (they just happen to be called Falstaff and Prince Hal, but if you called them 'Sir John' and 'Prince Henry' it might be possible to accommodate this point!). More of this in a moment.

What in a minor author would hardly have been cause for comment, becomes in the case of Shakespeare a matter of intense concern. And things are further complicated by the fact that we have to rely almost entirely on the internal evidence contained within the plays themselves. We know so little that is really important about Shakespeare's working methods that we cannot say whether he would have adhered rigidly to a preconceived plan.

Let us imagine, for the moment, that there was to be only one 'Henry IV' play. You will recall that *1 Henry IV* builds to the tableau of Prince Hal at the Battle of Shrewsbury, bestriding the two corpses, real and presumed, of Hotspur and Falstaff. Hal has redeemed his honour and subdued his inclinations to self-indulgence and low life: he is ready, at this moment, to become the hero of Agincourt in the play *Henry V*. What more is there to say? There is no need for a *dramatic* version of history to deal with every detail; *Richard II*, for example, does not mention the Peasants' Revolt, and Shakespeare could have dealt with little matters of unfinished business, such as the death of Henry IV, in the opening narrative of Chorus at the beginning of *Henry V*.

Supposing this hypothesis were true, we would have to assume that what then intervened, was the real world of the commercial theatre. It is generally agreed, from such evidence as the number of printed editions of *Part One*—seven in all before the 1623 Folio—and the promises in the Epilogue to *Part Two*, that Falstaff was a tremendous popular success. In the same way that the film of *Dracula* led to a crop of similar films down to *The Hound of Dracula*, so *1 Henry IV* might have generated *Part Two* 'by popular request'. However, in spite of the Epilogue to *Part Two*,* Falstaff doesn't appear in *Henry V* (you will recall that he dies off-stage); this last hiccup is curious, and seems to upset the 'commercial pressures' theory, were it not for the usually accepted story that Queen Elizabeth was herself a fan of Falstaff, and insisted on his resurrection in *The Merry Wives of Windsor*.

If we accept this argument, then *Part Two* is merely a sequel to *Part One*. Many sequels are simply a repetition of the mixture as before and in this way fulfil the audience's expectations.

What major examples of repetition can you point to in *2 Henry IV?*

---

* See Dr Johnson on this passage: 'Let meaner authors learn from this example, that it is dangerous to sell the bear which is not yet hunted, to promise to the publick what they have not written'.

I expect you have mentioned that rebellion, only temporarily subdued by the Battle of Shrewsbury, flares up again. The play builds once again to a confrontation with the rebels, this time at Gaultree Forest, in Act IV. Prince Hal and Falstaff take part in the low tavern life, until Falstaff is required to recruit soldiers for the war. Henry IV goes on feeling guilty about things in general and laments his wayward son: one day he is going to sort things out and go off on a crusade (as mentioned in the first scene of *1 Henry IV*). Prince Hal decides to reform in a central scene of each play: *1 Henry IV*, III.2 and *2 Henry IV*, IV.5. What is particularly interesting is that, *in order to repeat the story of 'Hal's reformation'*, the newly-won honours and previous 'victory over himself' at the Battle of Shrewsbury are soon lost sight of, and the king cannot rid himself of the idea that Prince Hal is 'wild' and unsuited to be the heir to the throne; he goes on believing Hal to be unregenerate until he is almost at the point of death.

Other kinds of repetition are more subtle, however, and could well be used to *oppose* the argument that *2 Henry IV* is merely 'the same again'. Did you notice how the 'mock rejection' of *1 Henry IV*—

> *Falstaff* (*as Hal*) Banish plump Jack, and banish all the world.
> *Prince Hal* (*as King*) I do, I will.
>
> (II.4.465–6)

—is paralleled by the *real* rejection in *2 Henry IV*, and that the 'mock Assumption of the Crown' in the same scene is in some sense an anticipation of the *real* assumption of the crown in *2 Henry IV*?

Now re-read Davison's Introduction to *2 Henry IV*, pages 8–10 and 26–34. What is his view of the relation between the two plays?

He says of *2 Henry IV*: 'that it is very different from *1 Henry IV*' (page 7) and that it is '*not* a sequel' (page 9). Instead he gives us the very interesting idea that it is a deliberate contrast to the First Part (page 9). He prefers to call Hal 'Prince Henry' in the second play (page 26 and see also page 17), and he stresses throughout the Introduction that this is a 'colder' and 'sourer' play. He makes a great deal of the changes that have come over Hal and jolly Jack Falstaff of *1 Henry IV*, contrasting these characters with those of Prince Henry and the 'evasive' and 'declining' Falstaff of *2 Henry IV* (pages 26–34).

If we reject the idea that the Second Part is merely a sequel, and wish to argue that *Henry IV* was planned in two parts from the beginning, we shall need to consider another approach to the problem which involves going beyond the set plays in this course. Shakespeare's History plays, or to be specific, those which deal with the fifteenth century, are arranged in sequences, which are sometimes described as 'tetralogies' (groups of four plays), though this is not, of course, Shakespeare's own terminology. The first of these sequences to be written was concerned with the period after 1425, and includes *Henry VI, Parts One, Two* and *Three*, together with *Richard III*; this seems to have been planned as a whole, and though Richard III is such a dominant character that his play is usually seen in isolation, his reign is the culmination of a long process of civil disintegration—the Wars of the Roses, if you like—which is destined to lead to the establishment of the Tudor dynasty in the closing scenes; it is made fairly clear that the Tudors are God's solution to England's woes.

The *Richard II, Henry IV Parts One* and *Two, Henry V* sequence, though written later, deals with the earlier part of the fifteenth century: Richard II, the last king to rule in England by direct descent from the Plantagenets, is deposed by Bolingbroke, who 'seizes the crown' to become Henry IV, Henry is a usurper, and dies with the guilt of his crime still unpurged: his last long speech includes the lines:

> . . . God knows, my son,
> By what by-paths and indirect crooked ways
> I met this crown . . .
>
> (*2 Henry IV*, IV.5.183–5)

the word 'met' conveying a wealth of meanings and evasions. Henry IV's illegal and tricky position (he has been played as a 'Nixon' figure during the early 1970s) is one of the reasons why the disaffected nobility continue to conspire in both the *Henry IV* plays and at the beginning of *Henry V*, and serves to explain why the rebellion is blessed by the Church (*2 Henry IV*, I.1.189–209). Nevertheless, and this is very important in trying to understand the *sixteenth-century* reaction to these plays, even worse kings than Henry IV, for example Richard III, were thought to have been placed on the throne by God to be 'His scourge and minister'; the plays have to teach—in the political climate of the 1590s—that rebellion is never justified. Historically, the Tudors, whose claim to the crown was weaker than that of Henry IV, never seem to have felt secure, and plays about deposition were capable of being construed as incitement to rebel: *Richard II* was apparently put on by the players at the time of Essex's rebellion, and Elizabeth's famous remark, 'Know ye not that I am Richard II' illustrates her sensitivity on this issue.

A counter-movement to the theme of Henry IV's guilt is provided by Prince Hal, who is referred to, or appears, in all four plays. His 'muddy' youth reminds us of the folk-tale of the least likely son who eventually becomes a prince: ultimately he will be converted and in *Henry V* lead the nation to conquer France with God's blessing. That is to say, he will be the audience's ideal of a king; those of you who know the later play may well feel that Shakespeare himself has certain reservations about Hal/Henry V, but at this stage I only want to point out the major themes of the tetralogy.

The whole sequence also evinces a major shift in tone, from the medieval ceremony surrounding the divine King Richard to the post-medieval world of realism and modernity. Henry IV is usually seen as a 'workmanlike' and pragmatic ruler; Henry V's greatest moment, as presented by Shakespeare, is when he walks the English camp in disguise the night before Agincourt. It may be that his previous low life escapades with Falstaff enable him now to converse idiomatically with the English troops and so show himself to be a leader who is truly in touch with the people.

A more technical aspect of the relation between the *Henry IV* plays, which may also be put aside until you are more familiar with the conditions of the Elizabethan stage, is the exact status of the texts which have come down to us and their relation to plays on similar topics. Shakespeare rarely seems to have 'invented' his plots, and may have been asked to rewrite plays by other authors. (Such an explanation is often given to account for problems in the text of *Hamlet*.) In the case of the *Henry IV* plays we are in possession of an apparently earlier treatment of the same material called *The Famous Victories of Henry V*, which was put on by a rival company (see Davison's Introduction, pages 15–20). I don't wish to get involved in a detailed discussion of this inferior work, but simply ask you to consider the idea that the *Henry IV* plays could be seen as Shakespeare rewriting somebody else's play. Such a process of 'remaking' is both a help to the second author—the basic story is there—but also a hindrance in that he is presumably expected to keep to it. This evolution of the *Henry IV* plays from an earlier original could make us face the fact that not even Falstaff is entirely Shakespeare's creation, and is related to the Oldcastle of the earlier play. Furthermore, Falstaff and Pistol, as off-duty soldiers, are related to a well-known type, the *miles gloriosus*, the 'swaggering soldier' of classical comedy: notice how much more clearly Falstaff is a military figure in *Part Two* than in *Part One*. John Dover Wilson, in his famous study, *The Fortunes of Falstaff*, saw him as a development of the allegorical figure of Vice, or Riot, in Tudor Morality plays, a misleader of youth well-known to the original audience. While Shakespeare's absorption and total transformation of these earlier stage-figures must be conceded—Falstaff is always a 'real' rather than an allegorical character, surely; traditional styles of acting associated with such figures would influence the presentation of Falstaff upon the stage, and make his rejection—like that of the Vice—the expected climax of the play.

By way of a conclusion

IN the end many people have felt that, looking back over the two *Henry IV* plays, they have been in some sense engaged with a text of 'epic' dimensions; Schelling, for example, in *The English Chronicle Play* (1902), commented that the *Henry IV* plays presented 'the whole range of human life . . . in its political and social relations'. 'Epic' implies more than this, however, and it is often asserted that these plays enshrine the *national story* or *myth* to which Elizabethan spectators gave conscious or unconscious assent. After the ghastly turmoils of the fifteenth century the Elizabethans wanted to preserve the *status quo*—the Tudors had at least given them stability, though there had been a bad patch after the death of Edward VI. Epics are traditionally poems about battle and war, but even Homer had found room for the converse in the scenes of peace depicted on the shield of Achilles; and so, in this play, the apparently superfluous Gloucestershire scenes may contain the real values which have eluded the rest of society during the 'unquiet reign of Henry IV'. Here, to sum up, is a brief yet enthusiastic account of these two plays which emphasizes their epic quality.

> I suspected it at Stratford four years ago, and now I am sure: for me the two parts of *Henry IV* are the twin summits of Shakespeare's achievement. Lime-hungry actors have led us always to the tragedies, where a single soul is spotlit and its agony explored; but these private torments dwindle beside the Henries, great public plays in which a whole nation is under scrutiny and on trial. More than anything else in our drama they deserve the name of epic. A way of life is facing dissolution; we are in at the deathbed of the Middle Ages. How shall the crisis be faced? The answer takes us to every social and geographical outpost: to Eastcheap drunks and Gloucestershire gentry, to the Welsh and the Scots, to the minor nobility and the crown itself.
>
> There is much talk of death; to the king it comes as a balm, Falstaff sags at the mention of it, Shallow is resigned to it, and Hotspur meets it with nostrils flared. The odd, irregular rhythm wherein societies die and are reborn is captured as no playwright before or since has ever captured it. In Hal's return to honour and justice the healing of a national sickness is implied. Implied: that is the clue—for there is no overt exhortation in these plays, and no true villain, no Claudius or Iago on whom complacent audiences can fix their righteous indignation. Hotspur is on the wrong side, yet he is a hero; Prince John is on the right one, yet his cynical perfidy at the disarmament conference would have astonished Hitler. Only a handful of plays in the world preserve this divine magnanimity. To conceive the state of mind in which the Henries were written is to feel dizzied by the air of Olympus.
>
> (Kenneth Tynan, 'Review of *Henry IV. Parts 1 and 2* at the Old Vic' (1955), reprinted in *Tynan on Theatre*, Pelican, 1964, p. 45)

Looking ahead

Let me have men about me that are fat

(*Julius Caesar*)

AS we move on to the study of later plays, you may find it useful to contemplate a Shakespeare, who, without mere repetition, was able to develop certain interests which first excited him the the *Henry IV* plays. Indeed, the format of 'the History play', perhaps brought to a careful perfection here, provided a model for the varied scenes of later comedies and tragedies. Consider Prince Hamlet's adept handling of the modes of discourse, and Shakespeare's disposal of the prose and verse scenes in *Hamlet* the play. On the other hand, 'the History play' also provided a tight organization from which Shakespeare learned to depart, especially in the looser arrangement of *Antony and Cleopatra.*

In 'the Roman History play', which we come to next, there are to be found many resemblances to the situation in the *Henry IV* plays. Since the anointed king—Richard II—had been deposed and murdered, Henry IV and Northumberland engaged in a bleak and naked struggle for power: similarly, the assasination of Julius Caesar produced a situation in which the Roman Empire was 'up for grabs'. In *Antony and Cleopatra* 'the world' is divided between military leaders; and I would simply draw your attention to the obvious similarities between Octavius and Prince Hal. Both are the heirs to empires, and have certain traits of personality in common. Antony, on the other hand, is known as 'a reveller', and this Falstaffian trait increases his 'humanity'. In both *2 Henry IV* and *Antony and Cleopatra* anarchic or 'holiday' propensities are rejected or defeated by business-like and organized officialdom: we observe what it takes to become a prince or a princess—but it is Antony who engages our sympathy in defeat.

Nevertheless, even when a situation is similar, Shakespeare never repeats a character: the nearest to a true *miles gloriosus* figure—Parolles in *All's Well That Ends Well*—is not like Falstaff, and, in *Hamlet*, Fortinbras is not quite like Hotspur. Finally, at the end of the course, you may like to consider whether there is anything in the suggestion that in *The Tempest* Caliban is a degenerate parody of Falstaff.

JP

Further reading

You will find an excellent and up-to-date list in the set book (*1 Henry IV:* pp. 39–42 and *2 Henry IV*: pp. 41–5).